Stellar Patrol Ranger

P.M. Griffin

SPEAKING VOLUMES, LLC
NAPLES, FLORIDA
2023

Stellar Patrol Ranger

ISBN 978-1-64540-925-0

As this is the last book Pauline Griffin wrote,
we her writing family would like to dedicate it to her memory.
Thank you, Pauline, for thirty-five years of fun and amazing fiction.
May your memory burn bright as the stars.

Chapter One

Ranger-Captain Taigue Murchu was in no good mood, but he paused to look at the office spire. It was well worth seeing, magnificent and beautiful, as were most of Aurora's structures.

By day, it was a fine sight, a seemingly immeasurably tall tower tapering gently to a needle point. Save for its square shape, it might almost be a giant's starship. Viewed now, at night, it was sheer magic. The window tints, dormant under the sun-star's rays, were activated by the artificial lighting. Each level was a very slightly paler shade than the one below it, and the eye followed the progression of color from the deep, dark orange of the ground floor to the delicate cream at the distant summit. It was a sight few visitors could readily forget, one few would wish to forget.

His eyes went to the clear, bright yellows of the center. Somewhere up there behind one of those windows sat the woman whose life he was about to disrupt. The Auroran Archopological Institute had its offices on the hundredth floor, he knew, but he was not about to count the levels up to it, and he did not know behind which of the windows on that level Doctor Lis was sitting. No matter. He would be there soon enough.

Passing through the arched entrance to a lobby of cream-colored marble, he flashed his identification at the security guards, holding it steady long enough for them to see it clearly. They waved him on, and he headed for the lift that would carry him up to his destination.

Perhaps this was a wasted errand. Banna Lis was not in either service, Navy or Stellar Patrol, that she should jump to aid him merely because he had need of her assistance. She might just consign him and his mission to one of the ultrasystem's more picturesque hells and show him the door.

He sighed. That was probably an injustice to her, he decided. Inner-system native though she was, if the humanity revealed in her writings reflected anything of the well-respected archopologist herself, she would not stand by unacting and allow people, innocent or otherwise, to be slaughtered. Her own family history testified that she could not. Her sister, Anna Lis, had answered the Navy's call and had enlisted to battle the Arcturian Empire, although she might have taken honorable refuge in her studies as her siblings had done. Aurora provided volunteers enough to permit her that privilege. Some of her strength of character must be present in this kinswoman of hers as well.

Taigue's mouth hardened as he boarded the lift. Sergeant Lis had died in battle less than two years previously. He did not want to be responsible for the same thing happening to her sister.

He roundly cursed himself, his commander, and the vacuum-brained surplanetary police on Gamma of Chadwick who could not hold onto their own property. The scientist's role in its recovery or destruction was supposed to be minimal, just get him to his destination and provide him with a cover for being there, but he and everyone else involved knew that to be so much moonlight. There was simply no such thing as minor involvement in any battle with space pirates. It stuck in his gut to drag a civilian into this business at all, much less when she would have to remain part of it for a fairly long period of time. She could too easily get herself killed, aye, and get him butchered along with her. His scowl deepened. This was technically not even his own proper work, though assignments of this sort came all too often in these troubled times. When they did, he preferred either to have capable backup or at least to be allowed to work on his own.

The lift stopped, and the Ranger stepped briskly though the doors as they opened. What he preferred was irrelevant. With lives at hazard, thousands of them, he had no other choice. He had to prevent what was an otherwise inevitable disaster, and he needed Banna Lis' help to do it. That aid he would have, however much he disliked being forced to use it.

* * * *

Banna's fingers glided over the entry pads of her computer, moving so swiftly and surely that they seemed almost to be acting of their own volition rather than obeying the direction of her will.

The list which materialized on the screen in response to her summons was long. It contained a great many small, even insignificant, entries, but she took no less note of those than she did of the major items. There was little chance of replacing forgotten specialized material of this sort anywhere on the rim of the vast Federation ultrasystem. On Ruby of Diamond, her ultimate destination, there would be no hope at all of doing so.

Satisfied at last that nothing had been omitted, she deactivated the machine once more and sat back, closing her eyes to rest them for a moment.

She had known everything was in order. There had been no need to make this final check, but Banna Lis was not one to omit any safety ritual when she prepared for an expedition. Caution and attention to detail were as essential to her peaceful work—and to her own survival—as they would be if she bore an active part in waging the great War rending the galaxy.

Only a few more hours to go. By this time tomorrow, she would be in deep space, on the first stage of the long journey that would take her to Diamond's planetary system and the world on which she was to base for the next several weeks, or for months if her delvings there proved as significant as she was anticipating they would. She had made her plans to permit an extended stay and hoped with all her heart they would be justified, that she would be able to unravel some small part of the secret of Ruby's past.

The woman gave a little sigh at the thought of the rugged, lonely time ahead of her. Even after all these years, something inside her still shrank from abandoning Aurora's civilized comfort for the primitive existence which was an archopologist's usual lot out in the field.

Banna's eyes opened again. In truth, she knew she actually welcomed the opportunity to get away. Her homeworld's elegant lifestyle was and would always be her choice when she had the leisure to enjoy it, but years of exposure to vastly different circumstances had subtly altered her. She no longer thought as did many of her peers here, and she too often found herself, at least internally, at variance with them. It was an uncomfortable, unhappy situation for her, one she was usually glad to escape when the time to go again came.

Last night's farewell dinner was a testimony to that. She had enjoyed it for the most part, had loved what had become a traditional gathering of family, friends, and associates coming together to wish her well on yet another of her long-term expeditions, but the evening had not been without its irritations. She could feel her annoyance rise again at the memory of her brother's casual discourse with his colleague, Samel Turpin. Both were learned men, highly regarded throughout the core worlds of the Federation ultrasystem for their theoretical work in comparative sociology, but she had wanted to scream listening to their talk about masses and movements and the lessons of history. –History? The pair of them had absolutely no comprehension of what history was.

Her dark eyes flashed. That was her work. History was no chronicle of dry dates and laws. It was the vivid story of countless individual men and women, the story of their lives and how they lived them, of their striving, of the legacies each and every one had passed on to those who had followed after them since human-level intelligence had first appeared in the universe.

She had kept her anger concealed and in check. This emphasis on humanity was basic to archopology, which labored to bring the long-hidden details of the epic tale to light. It was not realistic to expect every discipline would hold it in the same degree, much less hold it as passionately as she did, but by the Spirit of Space, no one should be oblivious to the basic human role, either. People were not soulless automata, and the tendency of experts in so many fields to summarily lump marvelously unique beings into arbitrary categories to support one theory or another would never cease to infuriate her.

The Auroran looked up and called out permission to enter as the sound of a knock interrupted the unproductive train of her thoughts. She quickly masked her faint frown. What could anyone want with her now? It was late, hours past quitting time. All loose ends in her office had been put in order, and she had made her farewells to just about everyone either last night or earlier in the day.

She did not recognize the man who stepped briskly into her office almost before she had finished granting him leave to do so, and she studied him carefully although unobtrusively, drawing on the experience she had gained in her travels to learn what she could about him.

The newcomer was either a Terran or one whose race held closely to prototype. He was fair of complexion with sandy hair and sharp, gray eyes that seemed to miss no detail of the world around him. His features were regular enough to be pleasing but were somewhat grim, bearing the stamp of one who carried responsibility and had carried it for a long time, perhaps too long. There was an air of quiet competence about him that she liked, and she thought he could command others as well as himself.

In build, he was slight, well-proportioned but wiry rather than heavily muscled. His carriage bespoke a military connection, hardly surprising in these troubled times, and he moved with a spacer's easy grace.

"May I help you?" the scientist asked. She spoke courteously albeit with a purposely bland expression. She was curious about this midnight visit but wary as well. A friend who had missed her earlier might logically come to see her now with some last-minute good wishes or a message, but she did not trust at all the motives of a stranger who found it necessary to do so.

"Doctor Banna Lis?" His accent was soft, not Terran, though she believed Basic was his mother rather than an acquired tongue.

"Yes. You have the advantage of me."

"I'm Ranger-Captain Taigue Murchu, currently based out of Deneva."

The woman's sharply winged brows lifted. "That is a long way from Aurora, Captain." He was also clad as a civilian, but she let the direction of her gaze make the observation for her.

Murchu nodded. "It is. –I apologize for coming to you at this hour, but I didn't want to approach you too soon."

Or to be seen making his approach, Banna thought. "If you had waited much longer, you would not have seen me at all," the archopologist responded with the rhythmic formality that characterized her own people's use of Basic. "You are doubtless well aware of that fact."

She motioned toward the straight-backed chair before her desk. "Please sit, Captain Murchu. I do not like keeping visitors at attention, and you might as well make yourself comfortable while you tell me what the Exploratory Force wants with me."

Banna waited until he was seated before speaking again. "I hope you will not think me uncooperative if I ask to see your credentials."

Taigue smiled. He liked rather than resented both her coolness and her caution. At least she had backbone and a full complement of brains. "I couldn't imagine your letting me get much farther without seeing them, Doctor."

As he spoke, he took the thin, shield-shaped metal plate from his shirt pocket and handed it to her rather than merely holding it up in front of her as he had with the security detail below.

The Auroran studied and then returned it. "Very well, Captain Murchu. I would still like to know what the Rangers want of me."

"A great deal, I'm afraid, in terms of tolerance. We've confirmed you've had no luck in finding a hand to perform the grunt work and general camp duties on your upcoming expedition. I'll take the job."

She looked at him in amazement. "Why in space do you want to go to a rock like Ruby of Diamond? She has absolutely nothing to offer anyone not conducting some sort of scientific research, at least not at this stage. Not only is she incapable of supporting unaided human life, but, she has none of her own, not so much as a stray virus. All you will find is an unstaffed planeting field and a couple of basic warehouses, one of them containing some emergency supplies and repair equipment."

"A great many individuals in this ultrasystem would view her isolation as a distinct virtue when coupled with her breathable atmosphere and Terra-normal gravity. A ship using any caution at all could readily slip in to drop or pick up cargo and lift again without alerting anyone on Sapphire or Emerald to her presence."

Banna Lis' eyes narrowed. "She would be carrying special cargo, of course?"

"Aye."

The archopologist straightened, mentally if not actually physically closing the interview. "I had best be frank with you, Captain. My work takes me to some of the most forsaken reaches of the ultrasystem and holds me there, usually alone or with a mere handful of companions, for long stretches of time. I could be in stellar-class trouble without the goodwill of the locals, which I can hardly expect to retain if it gets out that I threw my lot in with the Stellar Patrol on some antismuggling sweep."

"Keep quiet about it."

"That is the way the Patrol functions?" she inquired icily.

"If circumstances force it on us, aye. We do what we must." Impatience tinged his voice. "You regard any effort on our part to control illicit trading as little short of contemptible, I suppose?"

"My personal opinion is irrelevant," Banna responded. Her mouth hardened. "Nor do I imagine that my willing consent is of any consequence. You are prepared to force my compliance, are you not?"

The man nodded. "Planets not yet approved for colonization fall under Patrol jurisdiction. If you want to retain access to Ruby of Diamond and other worlds like her, you'll take me with you."

"There is nothing more for us to discuss, then, is there?"

Color rose in Taigue's cheeks. Lis might have been a physician addressing a flesh rot fungus spore viewed under her microscope. "Damn it to all the Federation's hells, Doctor, I'm as well aware as you that it's the special trading that's keeping a lot of colonies solvent, aye, and some of them alive, with the present difficulty in transporting legitimate goods, and you don't have to tell me, either, that it's the crews carrying them and the rest, not the Stellar Patrol, who are chiefly responsible for holding pirates in check in more than one rim Sector. I'm not going to all this trouble for a few cargos of untaxed opaline or mining gear. The War hasn't left the Patrol with either the personnel or the equipment to hunt down petty operations like that, nor would any of the planets in Diamond's system be a convenient drop for such material. They're too far off what pass for commercial starlanes out there."

An ugly, creeping horror knotted her nerves. "Raklik?" she hissed.

He nodded. "Raklik, plus all the related street drugs."

"Go on."

The Ranger-Captain leaned a little forward in his chair. "Four months ago, raiders hit three facilities on Gamma of Chadwick in a well-coordinated attack. They made off with specialized machinery and laboratory equipment from one, and equally specific pharmaceuticals and chemicals from the others. It was a daring, neat job, quick, clean, and flawlessly executed, obviously the product of long and careful planning. Any Commando unit would be proud to own it. The perpetrators were in and out almost before anyone knew what was going on."

"Inside involvement?"

"Naturally, but the two fairly certain suspects vanished before the attack took place." He grimaced. "Navy Intelligence has taken over the investigation, and Gamma's own military has belatedly instituted stronger safeguards, but everything the bastards grabbed is gone."

"Where does the Patrol come in if the Navy is in charge?"

"Federation fleets are starting to push the Arcturians back. High Command can't afford to draw away any significant part of our forces from that drive, not now, or we could lose all our gains and maybe the War along with them, but the stolen material represents entirely too great a threat for us to ignore. All of it has to be retaken or destroyed."

"So the Stellar Patrol was requested to drop everything and concentrate on doing that?"

"Exactly." His eyes met hers. "Once the pirates, or, rather, the ones who planned the raid, begin production, they will flood their selected targets with their output. Neither the Patrol nor the various surplanetary authorities involved will be able to stop the deluge, not completely enough nor rapidly enough."

Murchu placed his hands on the desk in front of him. They whitened under the pressure he unconsciously exerted on them. "The triumph, or initial triumph, of criminals is not the worst of it. You know enough about raklik to realize that. We're looking at a massacre. The profits will be immense, but so was the outlay needed to effect the raid and, presumably, to set up the manufacturing facility and distribution network. The perpetrators will be anxious to begin reaping the benefits as quickly as possible. Raklik production is a slow, tedious process if it is done correctly. The sons of Schythian apes won't have the patience for that. Maybe they can't afford to wait. Whatever the reason, they'll rush the first batches through. A lot of what they release will, as a result, be pure poison. Thousands, tens of thousands, will die."

"May the flesh rot off their living bones!"

The man stared at her. The archopologist's strong response was unusual for one of her race, although he would have expected nothing less from a denizen of one of the outer worlds. The citizens of rim and near-rim planets lived under the potential threat of attack by both pirates and by the soldiers of the Arcturian Empire, and they identified closely with the loss of life, labor, and hope inevitably suffered as a result of such assaults. The same sharpness of feeling was not generally found in the peoples of long-established inner-system worlds. Generation after generation passed in ease and physical safety had generated a sense of security that tended to block real empathy with the unfortunate victims. An indirect assault like this would hardly do so.

Some such tragedy might have touched Lis personally, of course. Aurorans were strongly represented in trade. She could well have lost a friend or associate, perhaps on Tatarina. Members of many races had been slaughtered there.

"People of importance to you died in some raid?" Taigue asked sympathetically.

"No." Banna gripped herself. "I have viewed the results of massacres more than once, ancient maybe but no less graphic for that." She scowled. "Terra boasts several prime examples. There is the mass grave of some five hundred women, men, and children, most skeletons despoiled of their hands and feet, which were presumably taken as trophies by their killers.

"I have seen the skull of a young woman that still bears the stone spearhead which caused her death. She died on her back, looking into the face of the man who drove the accursed thing home. —I cannot imagine the kind of mind which could have done it, and you can put a large store of credits down that I would have no pity for such a creature were I to judge his case. I consider the present-day subbiotics preying on our member planets and colonies and on the ships servicing them as something lower still, since I have actually come to know a little of those they are trying to destroy. I include those who deal in chemical poisons like raklik in the same category." Fire rippled in her midnight eyes. "Does that surprise you so much, Taigue Murchu?"

"It's not what I expected to hear," the Ranger admitted. He was silent a moment. "This is not the same situation as an outright raid, but you understand why we must use whatever means necessary either to get those chemicals back or to destroy them? Four months have gone by already. There can't be much more time left to us before they're used."

"I understand," Banna said, "but not what makes you implicate Ruby of Diamond out of all the planets in the ultrasystem. Suitable sites for hiding or delivering contraband of that kind must be legion, places without a Stellar Patrol base literally next door."

"There are," Murchu admitted ruefully. "Our intelligence people haven't been able to focus on any one candidate. Ruby is merely one of many with a greater than average chance of serving the raiders' purpose, primarily because she is rather close to Gamma for ships cutting across rather than following the regular starlanes. Those raiders took an immense amount of material, and they would have been eager to unload it as quickly as possible. My orders are to go in and discover if they are in fact using Ruby to store it all."

"One agent?" she demanded incredulously. "To search an entire planet?"

"We couldn't spare a team. As it is, it won't be possible to check out every suspect world."

"But this . . . this is Commando work!"

He laughed bitterly. "Rangers spend more than half their on-world time functioning as guerrillas these days, Doctor, although we get neither their equipment nor any shadow of their glory."

The woman looked at him strangely. "Glory? It that what you want?"

"Space, no! What I want is some backup. It's a forlorn hope. We don't get much of that, either."

"I very nearly refused even to give you a hearing," she said softly. "I am sorry for that."

He responded with a shrug. "It's a familiar reaction. Patrol agents know where we stand with a large part of the civilian public. We interfere with too many cherished activities."

The Ranger-Captain grew quiet again. This time, his silence held for several seconds. "I'll do my best to keep you out of it all, Doctor Lis, but if I do stumble onto anything, I could bring a lot of danger down on you."

Banna's eyes lowered, but they were steady when they raised again to meet his in the next moment. "I'll just have to accept the risk."

"It's only an outside chance," he assured her rather too quickly. "I wouldn't dare involve a civilian otherwise."

"You have just stated that you would do whatever is necessary to complete your mission," she reminded him. "It does not matter. I shall provide you with the cover you require. My sister died fighting the Arcturian Empire. I will not sit back and permit our own spawn to destroy from within everything she gave her life to defend, not when there is something I can do to prevent it."

Chapter Two

A sharp breeze struck Taigue as soon as he left the lobby of the office spire housing the Auroran Archopological Institute. It was chilly enough to cause him to raise the collar of his thin jacket, but it was invigorating, and he welcomed its freshness.

The air cleared his senses, but it could do nothing to lift the gloom that had descended on his spirit after the conclusion of the interview.

The Ranger scowled. He had accomplished his purpose, but he felt as if he had suffered a defeat instead.

So he very nearly had thanks to his mismanagement of the whole business. Why in all space had he not simply described his mission at the outset as he had originally intended to do instead of blowing up like a newly sworn cadet over a reaction he had fully anticipated? He might not enjoy suspicion and barely masked reproach, but it hardly took him by surprise at this stage in his career.

His expression darkened still further. His service was fighting a war as real and frequently as deadly as that being waged by the opposing battle fleets of the two great ultrasystems, yet Patrol agents often received more indifference or low grade hostility than willing aid.

That was the problem of the civilians, he thought savagely, not any fault of his comrades. Too many people were engaged in practices that were questionable at best, leaving them uncomfortable around those pledged to uphold Federation law. Meanwhile, the War had drained the Stellar Patrol of its agents and its resources to the point that all their limited resources were devoted to preventing the most major predators from ripping civilization apart. The Patrol had nothing left for checking minor—and at present useful—infractions.

His anger turned against himself, where it belonged. None of that had made any difference to the matter at hand, or it should have made none. He had done worse than lose his temper just now. Blackmail violated both the stern code of his service and Federation law on a major level, and threatening to remove her access to an entire planet came dangerously close to that. Sense of duty had compelled Banna Lis to agree to his demands, as it would have moved her had he proceeded according to his intended course. She would do what he wanted, but he would be damn lucky if he did not find himself standing before a judge at the end of it all. An Auroran was more than capable of nursing her outrage in silence until their task was done and then unleashing it on him in full force when they returned to civilization. Under the circumstances, she would be fully justified in doing precisely that.

The man's lips tightened. If she did charge him, he was finished in his service, whether he was actually convicted or not, and he would have smeared both the Stellar Patrol and the Exploratory Force at a time when they desperately needed the grudging respect they had managed to win and maintain over the War years.

He merited no better, he thought bitterly. Had he misread the woman, she might well have damned his mission, thrown her own work and future to the winds, and brought charges against him immediately. That fell within the scope of an Auroran's nature as well.

It was as if he had purposely sought to sabotage his assignment . . .

Murchu's breath released in a sharp hiss, and his pace slowed. So he had insofar as trying to make it impossible for the archopologist to agree to his proposal. An agent, Regular or Ranger, accepted peril for himself and for his comrades, but he had been trained from his first hours as a cadet to shield civilians from it. He would readily have sacrificed his life to defend the woman's, and subconsciously, he had tried to do just that, to destroy himself in order to keep her safely out of the whole potentially deadly affair.

There was a greater chance of running into trouble on Ruby of Diamond than he had indicated in his description of the mission to Banna Lis, greater than his own briefing had indicated. Of that he was certain. He was not accustomed to bungling his assignments as he had this interview, and he had gained a reputation as a troubleshooter, one who could be depended upon to take on a rough situation and conclude it to the Stellar Patrol's satisfaction. If suspicion against Ruby were not strong, he doubted he would have been the agent sent there, and when he planeted, he was fairly sure he would find something significantly amiss. Anyone traveling with him, covering for him, would perforce be involved as well.

His commander had no more liked bringing in a noncombatant than Taigue did, but they had precious little, nothing in point of fact, to give him a start on his hunt. Everything would have to be done on-world, and the planet's lack of development, coupled with the short time they believed they had left, made it essential that he go in with some sort of ruse to cover his activities. To set down in the wilderness and explore it alone would take far too long. He had to planet openly at Ruby's sole excuse for a spaceport where he would have a chance of picking up some shadow of a clue about recent activity, licit and otherwise. To do it, he needed a legitimate reason for being there. If he lacked that or failed to carry it off, and his enemies were actually on-world . . .

He forcibly turned his thoughts to the archopologist herself. Doctor Lis was a striking figure in every sense. Her achievements and influence in her profession were enormous despite the relatively few years since she had earned her doctorate, and her name was known well beyond its circles thanks both to the real literary quality of the reports she published and to the intensely human emphasis of her work.

She was scarcely less remarkable in her person than in her accomplishments. Banna was of only moderate size among her own, but her people were a tall race, and she fully equaled him in height. Her build was slight, so slight that she seemed to have no muscle at all, an illusion quickly dispelled by her proven ability to function effectively and efficiently in a variety of rough, wilderness-class sites throughout the Federation.

Lis' features betrayed the Terran origin of her kind, those first-ship colonists who had planeted on Aurora and made her their own in the distant past shortly after the exploration of the stars had begun. They were finely formed and proportioned, very nearly meeting the motherworld's prototype ideal.

Her complexion negated her beauty in traditional Terran eyes. Her skin was starkly white and semitransparent so that the surface network of veins sustaining it were visible through it. The copper flame of her hair looked jarring in contrast.

The eyes were even more striking. Large and black as interstellar space, they dominated her face and her entire being. The power of them held him as strongly now in memory as they had earlier in the flesh.

They had been cold, those eyes, and superior even when the contempt had gone out of them. That expression, the distance it created, more even than the poised dignity of her bearing and the cool, white skin, had made her seem more an exquisite sculpture, a figure fashioned out of crystal or glacier ice, than a living woman.

The Ranger-Captain sighed and brought his mind back to the time ahead of them. He was still opposed to her involvement, but at least fate did not seem to have been totally unkind in choosing Banna Lis for this unwelcome role. She had accepted its necessity without force or prodding, and if she was not battle trained, she was at least somewhat experienced in the ways of wilderness worlds. In truth, she could probably do more for him than provide him with a passport on-world. This was her second expedition to Diamond's system, and her practical experience might well prove highly valuable in the work ahead of him. As for the rest, responsibility for their safety lay with him, and he did not intend to fail in that charge.

* * * *

The voyage from Aurora to Deneva proved to be enjoyable despite Taigue Murchu's ever-present consciousness of how rapidly time was slipping away from them. For one accustomed to the Spartan accommodations on Stellar Patrol starships, life aboard the gigantic transgalactic on which they were booked seemed little short of hedonistic.

Budgetary considerations required Banna and her companion to travel cabin class, but the archopologist's professional and literary reputation was such that she suffered no social slight either from the crew or from the other passengers on account of her more economical quarters. She enjoyed access to every public portion of the great ship and full use of all her facilities.

Because she had courteously introduced Taigue as an associate rather than merely as a hand, he shared the same privileges, a freedom of which he had gladly availed himself. An officer of the Stellar Patrol's Exploratory Force was not likely to find himself in so enviable a situation again.

He returned to his familiar universe when they transferred to the small tramp freighter the Auroran had chartered to carry them from Deneva to their final destination, but even that part of the journey was not unpleasant. There was no pretense at luxury aboard the *Day of Glory*, but her crew were a friendly lot who were glad of their passengers' company. The time did not pass slowly, with much of it devoted to study, Banna in preparation for the work she hoped to do, Murchu to familiarize himself as well as possible with the area in which he would have to operate.

At last, the *Day of Glory* entered Diamond's distant space, and her passengers retired to their minute cabins to strap themselves into their safety webbing.

The Ranger-Captain lay back on his bunk and gazed absently at the low ceiling. It would be some time yet before the freighter made her approach, but he could not blame the spacers for ordering them to secure themselves now. This was a busy time for a starship's crew, and he would not have appreciated having extraneous people cluttering an already cramped bridge were he in their position.

To occupy himself, he began to review mentally some of the distressingly sketchy information at his disposal about the little sun-star and her satellite worlds.

Diamond was a small, merry yellow star with a clutch of six whole planets and a narrow, dense asteroid belt.

Pearl, the innermost world, was tiny and perpetually shrouded in the swirling white clouds which had inspired her name and were responsible for trapping their star's already too-generous heat, raising the surface temperature to a fiery 980°.

The next two were much farther out and followed orbits so close to one another that they only barely avoided doing each other damage during their closest conjunctions.

Plants covered Emerald's hospitable, warm surface in a thick living blanket. Even her ample seas were cloaked with aquatic growth so that she did appear green from near-space, or green and white, rather, for great masses of brilliantly white clouds marbled her atmosphere and the face she showed to visitors from the stars.

Sapphire, her sister, was a water world. There were no massive land masses, but she boasted a multitude of islands, many of them large, three nearly attaining continental proportions. Her climate was varied, much like that of the Federation's motherworld.

Both planets were completely Terra-normal, able to support and foster human life without extensive technological intervention. Rich in a multitude of natural resources and vibrant with nearly countless life forms, none of which had attained human-level intelligence, they were such prime candidates for colonization that the Settlement Board was pushing the exploration of them despite its chronic shortage of personnel and equipment.

A new urgency had come into such work during the past couple of years. At long last, there appeared to be reason to hope the forces of the Empire were beginning to weaken, that the dire War the two ultrasystems had waged for so long was drawing to an end and that the outcome would be favorable to the Federation. When the conclusion did come, the process of expansion would begin in earnest again, much intensified by the needs of the multitude of newly demobilized men and women who found themselves without work or a productive situation on the worlds they had left to join the Navy. Birth rates had risen everywhere in response to the horrific combat losses, filling the surplanetary niches left by those going off to fight. With the combat ended and war deaths no longer occurring, places had to be found for everyone, excess offspring and returning veterans alike, and there would not be enough openings. Too many former soldiers would find themselves adrift in the civilian universe. A hardly less major factor would be those people whose homes and former lives had been shattered. Immigration was an answer to the dilemma, the only real solution. Fresh planets had to be explored, and those found suitable would have to be approved to receive the prospective colonists desiring to begin anew on them. These twins were testing out so perfectly that they seemed more direct gifts from the Great Creator than products of natural formation.

By rights, Ruby should have been ranked beside them in desirability, except for the disaster that had befallen her.

The two outer planets differed little from most of their counterparts throughout the galaxy. Both were well-nigh as frigid as space itself and utterly inimical to unshielded human existence.

Agate was a gas giant, beautifully banded with the methane clouds comprising her atmosphere and held to her by her brutally strong gravity. Four unimpressive moons shared her near-space, a unique feature in Diamond's system, where she was the only world to be so attended.

Jet was small with a dark, heavily cratered, irregular surface and no perceptible atmosphere. Doubtless in future years, she would prove of interest to scientists in a variety of disciplines since each planet is a unique entity offering new puzzles and new answers to those seeking them, but for now, with resources so limited, she attracted little attention.

The same was true of the Nuggets, the asteroid belt which was the final major component of Diamond's system, although the question of its origin posed an intriguing mystery. The rubble, ranging in size from near-microscopic particles through one gigantic fragment eight hundred miles in diameter, could be debris left over from the creation of the star-system, material which for some reason or combination of causes had never been able to coalesce into a planet. On the other hand, there was just the possibility that it might be the combined remains or partial remains of two individual bodies, the interloper that had wrenched Ruby from her place and a sister world of hers which had avenged them both in her dying. The cohesiveness of the material tended to support the latter dramatic theory. It would require close study to resolve the questions surrounding the belt, and Federation scientists were eager to begin unraveling them as soon as conditions permitted them to do so.

Ruby alone of Diamond's six jewels had been afflicted with a tumultuous past.

For the most of her long history, she had traveled in close association with her sisters. She was colder, aye, because she was the farthest out of the three, but she still had received enough of her sun-star's warmth to fully utilize her rich atmosphere and plentiful liquid water. A variety of life forms had come into being there, not only life as Emerald and Sapphire knew it but intelligent creatures who had prospered under the blessings and challenges she had presented to her offspring.

Then chance, a tragic accident of cosmic proportions, had irrevocably shattered the course of her development.

Approximately 150,000 years previously, a planet-sized body had hurtled into Diamond's system from out of deep space, cutting directly along the path of Ruby's orbit. Her sister worlds had been on the opposite side of their star and so had avoided injury, but the ruddy planet had not been so fortunate. The two bodies had not actually collided, but the unhappy world had been wrenched out of orbit and driven several million miles farther from Diamond's light and heat.

Miraculously, Ruby had held together during the violent horror of the upheaval and its aftermath, although she continued to be wracked by almost constant massive seismic and volcanic eruptions over the next fifty thousand years.

More incredibly still, she had retained her atmosphere through it all, but even that astounding fortune was not sufficient to shield her creatures from the fate the shift in her orbit had made inevitable. There was no escaping the cold.

Diamond was still close enough that the air, the oxygen in it, did not actually freeze, but the average temperatures had dropped so low it could hold almost no moisture. As that precipitated out and the surface and subsurface water froze solid, Ruby became one vast snowscape, an unbroken, planet-wide glacier.

Her shimmering armor had not remained intact for long. Volcanic activity was severe and worldwide in scope. Great quantities of newly formed ice had melted under the searing fury of its discharges. This tore over the surface in enormous, short-lived floods which ripped away still more of the ice, leaving the bare ground exposed to the cruel mercies of the fierce, desiccating winds and to the destructive power of the microscopic amounts of moisture it still retained. Soil and heart-stone alike soon crumbled and were lifted up in monstrous dust storms that eventually covered the remaining glaciers and refrozen flood waters until all those countless miles of ice lay buried beneath deserts of sand and gravel or lava rock, and Ruby took on the deep rust color of the oxidized iron so prevalent throughout her barren landscape.

Neither plants nor animals had been able to stand against such overwhelming disaster. Most species had perished at once. A few had managed to cling to life for a time, some for an astonishingly long while, but in the end, only the ruddy husk of the world which had borne them in such promise remained, that and a very few mysterious ruins to draw people like Banna Lis of Aurora.

The Ranger grunted as a titanic hand seemed suddenly to press down on him. Patrol vessels, like those of the Navy, entered and broke planetary gravity chains with scarcely a tremor to trouble those they carried. That was not true of many older civilian craft, and this little tramp freighter had obviously not been the recipient of even the most minimal modifications to ease the transition. In these times, the masters of starships servicing the outer reaches of the ultrasystem put any spare credits they had into additional armaments and defensive screens, not into acquiring comforts for themselves or their crews. He would have to resign himself to several very uncomfortable minutes until they were actually on-world and at the end of this stage of their voyage.

One short leg remained. The *Day of Glory* would planet on Sapphire first. The supplies filling most of her holds and the mail she carried were her primary charter. Her master would unload that as soon as possible and collect his confirmation of delivery before continuing the voyage to drop off his two passengers and their gear.

Taigue would remain aboard the *Glory* while she was on Sapphire. A man who chose to bury himself on a hole like Ruby of Diamond for an extended period usually had good reason for doing so. He would not be expected to expose himself unnecessarily to unwelcome attention by the various Federation officials present on the test world, particularly since she offered nothing in the way of amenities to attract him. If the small on-world Patrol contingent needed to contact him for anything short of a major emergency, they would have to do it through Banna.

That had already been arranged. The archopologist had intended from the first planning of her expedition to disembark briefly on the blue planet to confer with the Settlement Board. They would alert her to any alterations in conditions on Ruby as well as to any information which might prove useful to Banna in her work. While there, she would also logically drop in on what passed for Stellar Patrol headquarters to report the arrival of her party and provide the coordinates of her proposed work sites on Sapphire's uninhabited sister world. His comrades would have ample time to tell her anything he needed to know when she did. Should there be reason to contact him directly, a party of them would board the freighter ostensibly to examine the archopologist's gear and supplies for possible contraband and speak with him there.

Chapter Three

A soft knock roused Murchu. He rubbed his eyes and sat up, wondering how long he had been asleep.

"Come in," he called.

Banna entered his quarters. The archopologist was clad in a simply cut tunic and trousers typical of those worn all along the starlanes. Her high boots were designed to support and protect her legs, and the corrugated soles promised good purchase on a variety of surfaces. Most of the pouches on the broad utility belt circling her narrow waist were empty as yet, but he noted that the holster was in place and the butt of a hand blaster protruded from it.

The nails of the hand resting casually on it were short and untinted, and she wore no color enhancements on her face, nothing but the inevitable layer of protective silicates utilized by all pale-complexioned travelers, himself among them, to defend themselves against light intensities stronger than nature had prepared them to bear.

The burnished copper hair no longer fell in a cascade of curls but was tightly pinned to her head in the braid almost universal to female spacers. It was no less lovely and little less dramatic for that reason, the Ranger thought absently as he raised his hand in greeting.

The man smiled at the sight of Banna Lis. She was a different being now from the woman he had first seen in her office at the Auroran Archopological Institute and later glittering in the rich salons of the transgalactic. Because he found the stark styles and vivid colors fashionable on her homeworld jarring, and because he was, in truth, more comfortable with the familiar, he thought the change an appealing one, though he doubted she regarded it as anything but a regrettable necessity.

The Auroran leaned against the frame of the door and surveyed him critically. "So this is how you pass the time while I am out playing courier for you?" she asked archly.

Taigue grinned and gave an exaggerated yawn. "Power down, Doctor. I don't doubt that you'll knock work in plenty out of my hide once we reach Ruby."

"You can put credits down on that, my friend. You demanded this job, and sure as space is black, now that you have it, you are jolly well going to do it."

He chuckled and motioned his visitor to take a seat on the space chest at the foot of his bunk, the only other piece of furniture in the coffin-like cabin. "Any news?" he asked, his mood sobering as he spoke.

Banna grew grave as well. She carefully pushed aside the nano reader he had set up there and sat down. "The Patrol informs me there are a couple of ships on-world at the moment." Her voice tightened as the fear she had been chaining freed itself and rose up in her. "Taigue, we were a long time coming. What if we are too late?"

He gently reached out to touch her arm. "You don't have to worry about that."

"I am not an infant, Captain!" the woman snapped. "I know the main production operation will not be on Ruby of Diamond, but the perpetrators may be getting drunk with the thought of the incalculable riches represented by those chemicals. They may well be tempted to prepare a raw batch or two to check out the process. The prospect might be just appealing enough for them to try moving them on one of the wealthy inner-system worlds, maybe even on my own Aurora."

"There isn't much chance of that."

"Not for Aurora maybe, given our comparative lack of interest in such products, and probably not immediately anywhere, but they, the planners, will have their eyes on a number of such planets," Lis continued desperately. "The inner systems are their prime markets, Taigue. You have to know that. Even with the pressure of the War, life is easy on most of them for the bulk of their citizens, and all of them have a portion of their populations addicted to some experience or substance, a tiny percentage of the whole but a significant number of individuals. Federation and surplanetary authorities have kept a tight control over raklik-class drugs, but there are too many other things to weaken minds and wills. The hunger for new stimulation, new pleasures, is too difficult for some to resist. Many of those microwits will leap at the opportunity to feel raklik's fabled roar. They will try that ill-prepared poison, and the massacre you described will occur on some planet or on several." Her hands balled. "Those bastards have to be ready to make some kind of a move soon, and even if we do reach Ruby and find them in time, how are the two of us going to stop them?"

The Ranger-Captain studied her for a moment. "You're stellar-class, Doctor," he told her quietly. "I've found myself matched up with far worse before now. We have reinforcements on call, but they are of necessity some distance away. Ruby's only one suspect of many, remember, and we can't have ships monitoring every one individually."

"Could your agents here on Sapphire not have taken a more active role in searching her?"

Murchu shook his head. "They've been going there as often as they can, but they have only three two-class fighters at their disposal. Their crew members are all well known, with such explicit duties, that they couldn't escape to conduct a search like this without calling too much attention to it. If the chemicals and equipment are on Ruby, they won't be neatly stacked in the spaceport. They're out in the wild lands someplace. We have to find them before we can try anything, and we have to work quietly until we do. Otherwise, their guardians would merely spirit them away. We'd never get our hands on them in that case and never secure any proof against the ones who snatched them. Remember, too, we may be watching or trying to watch Ruby, but we don't know who might be keeping an eye on Sapphire in return. Besides, our garrison here are Regulars, not Rangers. They wouldn't be as handy in a wilderness situation."

His jaw tightened, and he stared bleakly at the wall opposite him. "Even if what we want isn't on Ruby, the vermin responsible can't be allowed to guess how suspicious we are and how determined. If they suspect the government's coming close to them, here or elsewhere, they'll vanish. They'll know we can't watch the entire ultrasystem indefinitely. People capable of planning all this are also capable of waiting until it's safe for them to move again, and they will have the ability, the resources, to force their hirelings to wait for their promised fee."

Banna's dark eyes rested on him for a moment. She made herself shrug. "We shall have to take things as they come," she agreed. "Your associates here feel the job could not have been put in better hands."

Taigue could not quite quell his satisfaction. "They told you that, did they? Regulars probably wouldn't have mentioned it to my face, humble Ranger that I am."

"Childishness!"

Her companion laughed. "Granted, but it's another of those facts of life one just has to endure. I think even Commandos got their share of it in the beginning. Everyone holds them in near awe now." He sighed. "Don't be fooled, either, even by anything I may have said earlier. My real task is to find that contraband if it's on-world and then shout for help. Anything more dramatic is to be considered only in the event of dire need."

He flexed his shoulders. The sense of sleep was completely gone, but he had apparently been lying in a cramped position, and his muscles

28

felt stiff. "What about your own business?" he inquired. "Did you learn anything of interest?"

"Not really. There has been some spotty preliminary testing on Ruby in spare moments, trying out various transportation methods and the like, but nothing sustained. The Settlement Board chaps did drop off a couple of cams—a mutation of Terran camels—along with automatic feeders to see how well they adjust to the cold, but that's the only experiment going on at the moment."

"Cams?"

The woman's surprise died as it was born. No one could know a fraction of the creatures existing in the galaxy. She was familiar with the animals only because she had worked with them once before, several years back. "Cams are able to take a great deal more in terms of low temperatures and scarcity of water and fodder than their parent stock. Most of Ruby will always be too severe for them, of course, but they should have no problem adjusting in the equatorial regions. It is well worth the trouble of testing them, since they could represent a big saving in terms of fuel for fliers and transports, which will be at a real premium for a long time to come, should the suspected mineral deposits actually be located and prove commercially interesting."

"It sounds a bit savage to maroon the poor beasts on Ruby of Diamond from what I've learned about her," he observed, frowning. Rangers as a group tended to be ecologically minded and to give their sympathy and interest to the various creatures they encountered during their explorations.

Banna Lis laughed. "Not for cams. I have worked with them before. With their designated feeding schedule, the only abnormality likely to be discovered when they are collected in a couple of weeks is a dramatic increase in body fat."

"How are the tests on Sapphire and Emerald going?"

"Smooth as butterfly silk. Both will probably be receiving colonization approval within the year." She gave a little sigh. "Maybe Ruby can be given some of the attention she deserves then."

"Probably, particularly if it turns out that she has any minerals worth mining."

Murchu looked up as three sharp whistles on the signal siren announced the *Day of Glory* was preparing to go into space once more.

"You'd better strap down," he told his companion without enthusiasm, recalling their lift-off from Deneva. "We'll be finding some answers soon, maybe sooner than we'll like."

Chapter Four

The Ranger-Captain arrived in the *Glory*'s minute crew's cabin, that in which passengers and crew usually passed the bulk of their waking off-duty time, to find his companion already waiting for him.

"You survived again, I see," he commented. This planeting had seemed even worse than the one they had experienced setting down on Sapphire, probably because he had been anticipating its discomfort.

"I did," she replied, making a wry face. "I shall never enjoy this part of interstellar travel."

"Neither would I if I had to ride in these buckets all the time. Give me a good Patrol scout ship or cruiser any day.

The archopologist glanced toward the core ladder linking the various levels of the freighter. "We had best be going down. Now that he has delivered us to Ruby, Captain Jens must be getting impatient to be on his way again."

When Murchu neither moved to comply nor made her an answer, she looked sharply at him. "Is something wrong, Taigue?"

The man seemed to square himself. "Before we go any farther with all this, I want to make you the apology I owe you. I was navigating right off the charts back on Aurora."

Her expression softened. "Stand easy, my friend. I am not about to ream you for trying to protect me."

His head, which had been bowed, snapped up. "You recognized that?"

"Not at first," Banna confessed. "It took me a little while to know you well enough to realize what you had been doing."

"My way of protecting you could've rightly landed me in the galactic pen," he responded tightly. Then he studied her somberly, fixing his gaze on the blaster at her side. "Can you use that thing you're wearing, or is it meant for show?"

"I can use it on a range, but I have never been forced to fire it in earnest, not even against an animal."

"Leave any fighting that crops up to me if you can, then. You may instinctively hold back, to try to avoid killing. Our opponents won't have such reservations to slow them down."

"You are so adroit a butcher yourself?" she demanded testily.

"I've had to kill. At least, my inhibitions against firing at some son of a Schythian ape trying to burn me down have long since taken flight. —It's no boast, Banna."

"No. No, of course not. I am sorry, Taigue. It is just the tension—"

"I share that, I fear. I prefer to have a good, strong company behind me when I have to mix with raiders."

Murchu moved his hand away from his own weapon, realizing he was broadcasting his nervousness by keeping his fingers so near to it in here, where they were both patently safe from immediate attack. "Let's be on our way Doctor—"

The ship's intercom interrupted him. "Murchu, see me on the bridge."

Banna looked up in alarm. Was Taigue's cover blown?

She calmed herself. That was not likely, and it should make no difference to them aboard the *Glory* in any event.

"Go on up," she told him. "Leave checking out the flier to me. We can load it when you get back."

* * * *

The freighter's bridge was a cramped cabin in the foremost part of the crescent-shaped vessel, small in itself and so crammed with instruments that there was scarcely room for the pilot's and copilot's seats.

Marv Jens was in his customary place on the former flight chair. A short, dark-skinned space hound, there seemed to be little to distinguish him from the countless others of his kind roaming the rim of the ultrasystem until he took control of his vessel. Then the skill and studied daring which had kept him, his starship, and his crew alive in these poorly charted, nearly unpatrolled lanes became evident indeed.

Evident, too, was his sharp mind, and Taigue Murchu felt uncomfortable standing there under the scrutiny of those bright, black eyes. There was good reason behind this unexpected summons, maybe one he was not going to like.

Marv's expression did not change as he studied his passenger closely. That Murchu had been around, on-world and in space, was apparent. Everything about him testified to years of close acquaintance with danger, of surviving by his wits and nerves.

It was equally apparent that a good part of that time had been spent in one of the services. His carriage might as well have been a uniform so clearly did it proclaim the connection.

That was not a particularly encouraging sign. There were a lot of people out here on the rim whom the Navy had discharged for one sound reason or another, but there were also a great many who had taken their own discharge or who had been kicked out, often with a stop off in the galactic pen before being loosed on the ultrasystem again.

None of that was any of his business. What mattered at the moment was that Murchu seemed genuine in his adherence to the charter he had accepted from the Auroran archopologist. He had watched the pair since they had lifted from Deneva, and he had seen none of the signs of imminent betrayal. Whatever his reasons for wanting to bury himself on Ruby of Diamond, Taigue Murchu apparently intended to live up to the agreements he had made to get him here.

The *Glory*'s master pointed to the observation panels circling his bridge. Outside lay the paved saucer which was Ruby's planeting field, and beyond it, no very great distance away, stretched the rust red surface of the lifeless world.

Two other vessels shared the facility, both needle-noses, slender and graceful but with dark, pitted skins proclaiming the length of time which had passed since either hull had been thoroughly scrubbed. Both newcomers knew full well that the seeming neglect did not extend either to the starships' drive systems or to their ability to fight and defend themselves.

A knot of four individuals stood a little apart from the nearer craft, watching and apparently discussing the *Day of Glory*. It was hard to make out much in the way of detail between the distance and the four's cold-weather gear, but they looked to be precisely what could be expected to be manning those two starcraft.

"Friends of yours?" Jens drawled.

"No."

The spacer captain continued watching him. Taigue turned away from the panels. "I don't know any of the individuals, and I don't have any use for their kind."

"All right. I believe that. If I'd thought differently, I wouldn't have let you on board in the first place."

"So?"

"So I wanted to make sure. I would've had to let you off to join them if I'd been wrong."

There was little humor in Murchu's answering smile. "After making good use of me to be sure you'd get off-world again with a sound hide maybe?"

"Maybe." Marv straightened his thin frame. "Do you want me to lift now, with you two still aboard?"

"That's not my decision."

"Perhaps you should be the one to make it all the same. That boss of yours can handle my sort well enough and probably yours, but those chaps out there are a whole other crew."

The Ranger said nothing for several moments as he once more fixed his attention on the four watchers. "I'll talk to her, though I don't think it'll do much good. She's pretty set on getting back to those bloody ruins."

"Maybe we should stick around for a while, just in case you change your minds."

Taigue gave him a quick look of surprise. The usual reaction of a freighter captain to a nest of pirates was immediate retreat on all burners. That this man was willing to delay his departure for them was a measure both of his courage and of his basic humanity.

"No," he replied slowly. "I don't think it would be wise. If that lot wanted trouble, they'd have been on us by now. They probably wouldn't have let us planet at all. Since they've left us alone thus far, it's likely they want to stay quiet themselves. My guess is they're not really afraid of an inspection should you call one down on them before they can lift." Either that, or it was what they wanted the newcomers to believe.

"Innocent as babes, eh?"

Murchu shrugged. "If they're carrying no contraband at present and their papers are in order, which a pirate's inevitably are, what have they to worry about? The Patrol can't do anything to them." He was on familiar ground here. It was a situation that had foiled his regular-service comrades more than once during their seemingly never-ending war against the raiders. "For the same reason, I'm pretty sure they'll leave us alone, especially since we won't be hanging around the port area. We're not carrying any valuables, as they'll realize as soon as they question us, which they will do, and killing us would cause more problems than it would cure. An isolated party like ours reports in to some home center if not to the Stellar Patrol itself very frequently, and any lapse in communication would bring a rescue party on-world fast, a strong one with reason and authority to do more than ask a few questions and check documents."

"You could as easily be reading it all wrong," Jens reminded him.

Taigue touched his blaster. "I don't look for trouble. I try to duck it when I can, but sometimes it finds me anyway. I've managed to stay around this long despite that fact."

Marv eyed the plain, businesslike grip which seemed to slip of its own accord into his passenger's caressing fingers. He had not doubt the weapon had been put to the deadly work it was designed to do on more than one occasion.

If so, it had been used only when and with the degree of force necessary. This man was no shooting star, nor did he seem to be careless of human life. "Have it your way. I don't know if any good fortune remains on Ruby, but I hope it falls on you two if it does. You're going to need whatever you can get in the way of help."

"Thanks, Jens. I won't forget this."

That, he would not do, Taigue promised himself, not if he survived the assignment. Marv Jens merited at the very least the not inconsiderable advantage of having a Stellar Patrol officer for a friend. If Murchu had his way, there would be a more concrete reward as well. The *Glory*'s master had earned it given the risk he had been willing to take on their behalf.

He left the freighter captain and hastened to join his companion in the cargo hold. Banna Lis was no Loren ghost lily, but he did not want her loading the flier by herself, as she was likely to start doing once she finished checking it over. That was supposed to be his job, handling the muscle work on the expedition. He was not likely to have much time for it given the enormity of the task before him, but whatever would be possible, he was determined to do.

Chapter Five

The archopologist had already manhandled a couple of crates into the machine, but she stopped working and straightened up when she saw him. "Great timing, friend. –What did Jens want?"

"To convince me to talk you into our lifting with him again. There's a reception committee outside, and they're a bad-looking lot from what I could make out of them."

"It seems he might have brought that up with me directly."

Taigue smiled and leaned back against the flier. "Power down, Doctor. Spacers think highly of their own kind, but they see bone diggers and other scientific and scholastic types as decidedly lacking in some pretty basic survival skills."

Rather unexpectedly, her annoyance faded, and she smiled in her turn. "I am well aware of that. It has proven to be a rather useful misconception at times, as a matter of fact, so I should not complain now."

The Ranger's head lowered. "I've been thinking, Banna. Jen's right. You'd do better to go back with the *Glory*—"

"Stow that debris where it belongs, Captain. First off, if I do not stay, you no longer have an excuse for remaining. Secondly, the Institute is not exactly manufacturing credits in any of its labs. If I pull out now and wait for an all-clear, I shall probably not have the resources left to complete my work, and it will be a long time before I can mount another expedition." She frowned. "You do believe we have a good chance, do you not?"

"Aye, of course. We'd abort otherwise and come in some other way. Our suiciding outright would accomplish nothing. –I can work out something else, Doctor. Patrol and Exploratory Force agents either learn to be resourceful or they don't live very long."

The woman silenced him with an impatient wave of her hand. "Neither of us has any other acceptable option. Stop dissipating energy fighting a given and put it to some more productive use."

Banna's tone was weary rather than sharp. Murchu naturally did not relish the idea of walking out there to greet those pirates, but she realized it was concern for her and not fear for his own safety which was driving him to try to evade that need. He had not anticipated actually planeting in the midst of their enemies, and all the instincts honed into him during his years with the Stellar Patrol revolted against exposing a noncombatant to so immediate and direct a confrontation. His logical acceptance of the fact that he had perforce made her an equal in the endeavor would be small comfort in the face the upcoming challenge.

She took a deep breath and held it for several seconds, then she compelled herself to smile. "We are letting ourselves get spooked, my friend. Those spacers outside might not be innocent of all wrong, but they still could have no part in the matter concerning us and no interest in troubling a pair of strangers. Why not see how matters develop before we look for a war?"

Taigue shook his head, acknowledging defeat. "I yield, Doctor. Let's get this stuff of yours packed. I can double back on the sly later on if I must study the situation more carefully, but for now, I don't want any long delays in port once we get our introductions out of the way."

* * * *

Murchu wiped his sleeve across his forehead to take off some of the sweat. That was the last of their baggage, and to his mind, they could not have finished stowing it soon enough.

The woman was also half-sitting, half-leaning on the loaded vehicle. It gave him a perverse pleasure to note that she looked no fresher than he felt. Small wisps of hair were plastered in thin, vivid lines on her forehead and temples. Her hands and face were streaked with grime, and her breath was still coming in short, sharp gasps, although it was settling into a more normal rhythm again even as he watched.

"You do this by yourself?" he inquired incredulously after giving himself enough time to be certain he had full control over his voice.

"Naturally. I have no option but to do it when I cannot hire help. I just take my time with it."

"I should have known you were a madwoman when you agreed to take me on," he muttered. "And we still have to unload all this stuff when we reach your base camp."

His eyes darkened as he studied the tightly packed machine. "It's too much of a load, Banna."

"I know," she agreed. "Normally, we would bring only about a third of that with us and warehouse the rest for pickup as we needed it, but I am afraid to risk doing that with these others around. If they stole or destroyed our basic supplies, we could have a hard time of it regardless of how quickly we might expect a rescue party."

"Smart thinking." The Exploratory Force service taught its agents the wisdom of looking carefully to their own needs and leaving as little as possible to chance or to the efficiency of others, a care that was little short of law with respect to assignments on inhospitable planets like Ruby of Diamond.

He studied their transport with a practiced eye. It was a big civilian flier, a workhorse designed to facilitate life on a rural, undeveloped world rather than to ferry passengers around in a more urban setting. Cargo space was generous with only a single cramped seat for the driver and one companion. The engine was located in the blunt nose and vented through the tail. Conservative wings flanked the exhaust area. The long, narrow shape aided flight, as did the fact that the large wheels were deeply set into the body of the vehicle so only a quarter of their surfaces protruded, cutting the amount of air drag they created. It was an efficient, dependable vehicle, one whose like, in a large selection of models and variations, were in nearly universal use throughout the numerous planets of the Federation.

Unconsciously, he shook his head. Despite its versatility and strength, there were limits to what the machine could carry, and it was burdened well beyond capacity now. Although each crate and cylinder had been carefully packed to make the best possible use of the space available, the archopologist's supplies were piled so high that they had to be roped down to secure them, too high to allow the closing of the canopy. Even part of the limited passenger space was taken, leaving only barely enough room for the two humans.

He shook his head again, this time consciously. It would never fly. Even if the engine could manage to raise the machine a few inches, he would not dare to so much as allow it to hover in this state. The chance of a crash would simply be too great.

Their level of travel was not their sole concern, either, Murchu thought grimly. They had more than excess weight and enforced confinement to the ground to worry them. They were starting out with another significant check against them.

"Those wheels are bad planning," he said aloud. "They're too narrow for a loose surface."

"We should have no problem," the Auroran assured him. "Nearly all the desert between the port and my dig is solid ground, either lava or hard gravel. There is very little sand, not enough of it to mire us if we move carefully."

"We won't be able to do much else," he replied, relieved. "We're not going to be slipping into stellar drive carrying this load."

Taigue reached for his outer gear, which he had piled on the flier's nose before they had started work, and began pulling it on. "That's about it, I suppose. We might as well go introduce ourselves to Ruby and her other visitors."

The woman's things were beside his. He made a ball of them and tossed them to her. When she had readied herself to face the planet's numbing cold, he opened the driver's door with a flourish and motioned for her to enter, then went to the controls activating the hatch locks and ramp.

Chapter Six

The loading ramp descended smoothly. The Ranger-Captain waited until it had reached ground level, then locked it in place and signaled Banna to bring the flier out.

He watched impatiently as it nosed its way through the tight opening. He wanted to get this part of the disembarkation over as quickly as possible. It left both them and the *Day of Glory* too vulnerable to attack, although he knew Marv Jens had his lasers trained on the hatch even at this moment. They could not be fine-aimed on-world, but they would provide cover enough to permit a rapid departure in case of necessity. In any event, Murchu realized the spacer captain was eager to escape this threatening situation and would lift as soon as he saw his passengers were on the ground and at least apparently secure.

Lis gave a sigh of relief when she leveled off at last and came to a welcome stop on the hard pavement of the planeting field. It had not been a pleasant feeling creeping down that steep, uncomfortably slick incline even with Taigue's guidance to help her.

After raising her hand in a gesture of thanks to him, she looked about her at the little she could see of the desert planet that was to be her base and home for a minimum of several long weeks.

Her first reaction, in spite of her previous visit here, was a sensation of shock. It was natural enough. Most worlds where humankind ventured had skies of some shade of blue or blue-green, but Ruby's atmosphere held so much of the ubiquitous red dust that it was a distinct and astonishing pink.

The particles were too small to interfere with breathing, but the perpetual cold made the air seem thin and hard to draw, though it was in truth almost identical to Aurora's in both pressure and oxygen content.

Only for a moment did her attention remain with Ruby herself. Her eyes fixed on the two dark vessels sharing the planeting field with the *Glory*, and forewarned as she was, her heart froze in its beat.

The Ranger came over to her. "What do you think of the neighbors?"

"I never saw one of these before." Not physically, but she had viewed ships like these on nano, both fiction and documentary, often enough to identify them for what they were. Five-class fighters were sleek, fast battlecraft highly favored by the wolf packs infesting the galaxy because of their speed, armament capacity, and efficient use of the proportionally large volume of fuel they carried. The condition of their skin confirmed the identification.

"You're fortunate there. The last time I set eyes on one, she was trying her best to blow me out of space."

"How were you able to see her?" the Auroran asked curiously. "I thought the members of the Exploratory Force had to strap down and stay out of the way during space action."

"Not when it's one's own scout ship that's being attacked," he replied dryly.

Color momentarily suffused the stark white of her face. The little fighters, which carried a crew of only two, had been designed specifically to meet the Rangers' needs, enabling them to get in and out of sites too small or rugged for larger craft and freeing them from total dependence on the hard-pressed Stellar Patrol fleets for their transport. "Sorry, Taigue. I had forgotten about those."

"No matter. I'd have been happier if those particular raiders had suffered a similar lapse in memory. They gave us a pretty bad time." A cold satisfaction touched his voice. "As it turned out, they were the ones who wound up regretting our meeting."

Banna Lis just nodded. There was no need to ask the pirates' fate. Duels in space almost inevitably ended in the annihilation of one of the contestants and all aboard her. Raiders, she knew, usually tried to avoid open combat for that reason, preferring to sweep in quickly by surprise and disable their victims before the crews could bring their defenses to bear. There was no profit to be had in blowing a freighter and her contents to space dust. It was only in the case of some private feud or in an instance like Murchu had experienced, when the chance to take out a lone and apparently significantly weaker Patrol ship presented itself, that they would choose to fight. Other times, they were forced to do so either by an intended victim's readying her defenses sooner than anticipated or because they faced capture themselves—and with it the near certainty of execution.

Her black eyes hardened momentarily. Battle took place more often than not, whatever the pirates' desire. The crews of attacked freighters always fought if given any opportunity at all. They had no choice. Death, often in slow and unpleasant form, or slavery of one sort or another, was the fate of everyone unable to provide a significant ransom who was unfortunate enough to be captured alive by those renegades.

"Here they come," Taigue hissed between clenched teeth. "Have your blaster ready, but keep it under your jacket where they can't see it."

He had known they would come soon, he told himself as the four spacers who had been watching the *Day of Glory* made their way toward them.

All were warmly clad, though none wore garments specifically designed for low-temperature surplanetary work such as he and Banna had on. That meant their business on Ruby was not expected to hold them long or take them very far from the spaceport.

None of them had face masks on despite the bite of the moderate breeze, and he could see that three, two men and a woman, were Emirites. All of those had whips, the signature weapon of their race, coiled at their waists close to the inevitable blasters. The fourth raider was an Albionan.

He tried to steady himself as his fear pulsed high enough to threaten to take control of him. Soon now, he—and Banna Lis—would learn whether he had misread those vermin or not. If so, his mission was probably at an end. He might or might not be able to take out these four before they got him, but there were another six, the crew of the second ship and the remaining hand from this one, around somewhere, probably watching from one or both of the fighters or from one of the warehouses. They unquestionably had their blasters trained on him.

As soon as they were within hailing distance, one of the group, the woman, called out a greeting, which he answered with a casual wave.

"You've got a heavy load there," the Emirite woman observed a few moments later when the newcomers reached the flier.

"That we do," the archopologist replied, "but it will lighten all too fast once we start using it."

Murchu was hard pressed not to gape openly at her. Banna's voice sounded natural, her smile and manner seemed bright and welcoming, as if she were talking to no one more deadly than a clutch of curious freighter hands.

Continuing the role of innocence she had assumed, she introduced both of them and casually described her purpose in coming to Ruby of Diamond, mentioning as well that this was her second visit to the planet, although it was only her companion's first. In answer to the Emirite's expected question, she replied she could not say definitely how long they would be staying. That depended entirely on the progress she made. She might even have to return on yet another expedition if

46

her labors proved particularly productive and she could not complete them before she had to terminate this one.

The Emirite woman said, "Why don't you two come in out of the cold for a bit? Have a chat."

Banna smiled at Taigue. "Go get a drink if you want one. There will be no chance for such diversions once we reach the dig. In the meantime, I shall take this thing for a few laps around the field to get an idea of how well it handles."

The Ranger nodded, although he eyed the four raiders warily. He could not pretend to share his employer's supposed ignorance and was bound to distrust the hospitality of such companions even if he had little real choice about accepting it. Any space hound would be aware of the folly of antagonizing or annoying them.

It was the reaction they expected, and one of the men laughed in a not-unfriendly manner, motioning him to join them.

Banna had done well. By anticipating the pirates' offer and displaying no fear of splitting her party, she had considerably reduced any suspicions they might have held.

"How'd she know there'd be anything to drink?" the spacer asked after they had gone a few paces.

"The doctor's been around enough to realize some comforts are going to be provided at every port whether official facilities have been set up or not. Her education's gotten that far even if there are still a few gaps in it."

"Just a few," he replied with a humorless chuckle. His small eyes narrowed. "Can't say I'd care to be stuck on this hole for long."

Taigue shrugged. "It's not so bad a charter. The pay's good, and a few weeks of enforced quiet won't kill a man."

"Especially if he doesn't want certain people to know where he is?" the woman interjected. "Like the Navy or Stellar Patrol maybe?"

"It could be downright beneficial under those circumstances," he agreed noncommittally.

She laughed and pressed him no further. By that time, they had reached the two warehouses, long, rectangular buildings about four stories high which stood out like lonely sentinels in the desolate landscape all around.

His guides pointed to the closer of the pair. "In there, friend. Everything a thirsty space hound could want. Our treat."

Once more, the Ranger-Captain could feel his stomach tighten. That could be an invitation to certain death. If they knew what he was, if they so much as suspected something, he would not leave that place again, but there could be no thought of turning back at this point.

He did not have to pretend to be ignorant of the perils he might be facing. A space hound on the run or a deserter, whatever his origins, would know full well the company he was keeping, and so he let his eyes travel suspiciously from one to the other of his hosts, as if measuring them and their intentions, before he pushed inside through the unlocked personnel door. Such a man would figure, as he had, that since the pirates had not struck already, they were not likely to do so now provided he continued to satisfy them. They were curious at this point, not angry or predatory.

Once inside, he found himself facing a cavernous chamber lighted chiefly by a large, centrally located skylight. It was as plain of decoration as it was empty of contents. Apparently, the emergency supplies the Auroran had mentioned were stored in the other building. It was not likely the raiders would burden their small vessels with such commonplace items unless their own stores were dangerously low. Ironically, in that event, they would have full right to take them.

The goods he sought were obviously not present, and there was no other room in this structure in which they might be kept hidden. The warehouse was designed to accommodate the massive machinery and prefabricated buildings which would be required should the planet be opened for colonization or other development, and despite its height, it consisted of this one vast space. It was probably the same situation in the other facility, given the ongoing danger of a sudden search by the Patrol or Navy seeking other, less sensitive goods.

Only in one spot, just to the left of the entrance, was there any sign of activity. A couple of camp tables and some chairs had been set up there along with an area heater which made the space around it tolerable if not actually warm, and a crate containing a honeycomb of cells holding a couple of dozen carefully packed cylinders. A second crate, this one unopened, stood beside it, and a number of mugs were lined up on the rough counter they formed.

Three more men and another woman, again Emirites, were sitting around one of the tables. The remainder of their comrades were doubtless keeping watch on the *Glory* and the world outside.

His party claimed the remaining table, all but the woman, who introduced herself as Cass. She gathered five mugs and a pair of cylinders. One of these, she opened at once and carried to the table along with the mugs. She poured out its contents, measuring each allotment so precisely that she might have been using an automatic dispenser instead of her eye. The portions were decidedly generous. When each had his share, she took a long drink from her own cup.

Her grimace warned the Ranger to brace himself before taking a more restrained swallow. Despite his care, he very nearly choked as the deceptively cool-looking liquid burned down his throat and seemed to explode as it hit his stomach. It was opaline, but there was no pretense of smoothness or quality here, just raw alcohol, quick-processed and unaged, meant only to do its work quickly and thoroughly. He would have to take it slow, he thought. He could handle drink as well as the next one, but if he were not damn careful now, he would find himself with drastically impaired reactions and fine-task capabilities just when he might need them functioning at optimum level.

Cass went to the counter and returned with the second cylinder. She wrenched it open and held it out to him. "Ready for a refill?"

Taigue put his hand over the mouth of his mug. "This is it for me. I've got to work when I leave here."

"Unfortunate for you," she retorted sarcastically. "You care?"

"If I crash that flier and incinerate our supplies, I'll be just as hungry as my boss," he answered calmly. "I wouldn't care a whole lot for that."

"You've got a point," the man to his right agreed.

There was a roar, muffled by the insulated walls around them but readily identifiable. A tremor ran through the Ranger-Captain which he took another sip to conceal. The *Glory* had lifted at last. Banna Lis and he were entirely alone in the midst of their foes.

"Looks like your friends are gone," Cass remarked.

Taigue shrugged. "There's nothing to keep them here."

Would that satisfy her? He believed the woman was a leader among the raiders, the mistress of one of the fighters perhaps. Convincing her he was harmless should secure both himself and Lis, or had the pirates only been waiting for the *Day of Glory* to depart before beginning their attack?

After a couple of tense seconds, his fear subsided as no move was made against him. This charade was about as subtle as these renegades got. If they were planning to kill him, they would do it now. With the odds so heavily in their favor, they knew—or would believe—there was nothing to hold them back.

That was not their intention, for the time being anyway. They seemed friendly enough, willing to accept him and his story at face value and to leave him and his bone-digging supposed-employer alone.

All except the Albionan. That one was not convinced. His eyes had remained cold, hard, his expression set, throughout the encounter, and his hand had never strayed from the vicinity of his weapon. It was apparent to the newcomer and to the raider's comrades that he neither liked Murchu nor trusted him at all.

Taigue pushed his chair back and got to his feet, moving slowly enough to telegraph what he was doing and so avoid startling the others. It would be best to end this masque as quickly as he could, before he said or did something to betray himself.

The Albionan moved, but more quickly still, before he could begin to draw, the Ranger's hand hit the grip of his own blaster with obviously practiced speed. "Easy on the drive, friend," he drawled. "This isn't the way I like to pay for a drink."

Their eyes locked and held a moment before the other man's hand slid back to his side.

Murchu willed his nerves to steady. That had been close. Had he been forced to draw, he would have been in trouble. The rest might not be particularly hostile to him, but it was unlikely they would just watch while he burned down one of their company. His gaze ran from one to the other of them, as if questioning, but all he read was indifference and a couple of grins. Apparently, the Albionan was a habitual shooting star or else had managed to get on his companions' nerves in some other way not serious enough to get him killed outright. At any rate, they were amused by his discomfiture now.

Moving at a discrete diagonal so he could keep an eye on his would-be assailant and the others, the Ranger-Captain walked over to the door and opened it a crack, enough so that he could peer out without allowing what heat there was inside to escape.

"The good doctor's back. She'll be wanting me to start earning my pay." He glanced over his shoulder. "I appreciate the hospitality. The fare's as good here as you'd find on Sapphire, and the company's better. A whole lot better."

"Patrol?"

He nodded. "Aye." That had been a gamble. Had the pirates not known about the base on the blue planet, he would have thrown a key card away, but he had been right in assuming a major operation such as he was hunting would have done its homework well. There had not been enough edge in the spacer's question to indicate real surprise or alarm. The man was fishing for information, trying to see how much he knew or if he would try to hand them a fouled chart.

"How many of them?"

Another fish hunt. They knew that if they knew the base was present. "Don't know. I wasn't moved to try to find out."

They all nodded, accepting what he said or seeming to accept it. Any other answer would have been strange in the extreme coming from the man he was pretending to be.

"Thanks for the warning," Cass told him. "We'll take care to planet in a more congenial port ourselves when we lift from here."

Chapter Seven

Taigue Murchu's shoulders ached with the tension stiffening them. He could almost feel a bolt burning through him as he strode away from the warehouse.

He kept his walk to a space hound's easy, ground-covering stride, not allowing himself to pick up speed as he neared outermost blaster range or to slow down or visibly relax once he had passed it.

The archopologist had seen him emerge and started out to meet him, leaving her vehicle where it was. The flier was patently not very maneuverable, a fact for which she was temporarily grateful, since it provided a handy excuse for parking it out of reach of at least their enemies' small arms fire.

Her pace was quick, impatient, and she reached the man shortly after he had passed beyond blaster range.

Her eyes seemed huge and impossibly black as they fixed on him. She, too, was holding her body and expression as if nothing were amiss, and no one watching them would suspect anything troubled her beyond an eagerness to set out, but he could see the deathly pallor underlying the natural whiteness of her skin. When close to her like this, her terror was almost palpable to one knowing her at all.

"Hold on, Banna," he whispered. "We're almost out of it."

"Praise the Great Creator you are all right." Her eyes closed. "I was afraid I had pushed you into a nova."

"Not at all. You played it just right."

He glanced at the flier as if that was what they had been discussing, and both of them started walking back toward it.

Taigue watched his companion out of the corner of his eye. "That was quite a performance, Doctor Lis. You bone diggers appear to have a few unexpected talents."

Banna gave him a tremulous smile. "There is nothing like wide-eyed oblivion to keep one out of trouble provided it is not carried to the ridiculous. We scholastic types learned that long ago."

He smiled himself to hear his own phrase tossed back at him.

The roar of a motor smothered the reply he had been about to make. Taigue whirled. A big flier was bearing down on them, firmly keeping to the pavement. The Albionan spacer at its controls.

Cursing, Taigue shoved the woman out of its path, knowing he was the primary target, then started running.

The machine gained on him fast as he reversed his course and made for the warehouse he had just left. The flier had issued from the second one moments before, leaving its vehicle door wide open. When it sounded as if it were all but on top of him, the Ranger spun around and, without breaking stride, raced for the vehicle itself.

He saw the attacker's expression turn from a vicious, triumphant grin to surprise and alarm even as he lifted the blaster he had drawn as the chase had begun.

Its beam was set to narrow for maximum driving force, and as he released the safety catch, he switched the control from stun to slay.

The flier was a civilian craft, a work machine totally unscreened against attack. His bolt struck the windshield point blank and tore through the fragments it left to slam into its target's face.

The burst was short. No more was needed. A fraction of that power would have done the job at this range, but he had not been certain the windscreen would not provide some modicum of defense, enough to give the Albionan time to duck and fire in his turn. Murchu knew he would not be given a second such chance in this contest.

He leaped for the now wildly careening vehicle and succeeded in catching hold of its side. He vaulted into it and scrambled across the seat to the driver's place. Shoving the corpse, which had slumped over the blood-drenched controls, aside, he brought the machine to a halt.

The port area seemed alive with running figures. Taigue raised his weapon again as people converged on the transport from several directions.

A broad brand of energy crackled along the ground. Banna! With less distance to cover than their foes, she had reached him well ahead of them.

She let off a second warning shot. "Back, all of you! Just remain where you are, and do not try anything with those blasters. –Taigue, are you all right?"

"Aye," he assured her, then raised his voice. "I have you all covered as well. Cass, you come nearer. Holster the firepower first. The rest of you, keep your fins planted where you are and stay quiet."

The fighters' lasers were almost certainly on them, but he did not think the pirates would fire. Not only did he believe his hunch was correct that the woman was mistress of one of them, but the rest of the raiders were far too close. They would almost certainly be hit as well if the starships struck. Weapons designed for use in space were difficult to focus for precise targeting on-world, and the loss of so many of their number would force the abandonment of at least one of the vessels and render the second all but impotent.

The pirates themselves were none too happy with their situation. They recognized their danger from the two strangers, but he doubted they would try anything, either attack or flight. They had seen enough of his capabilities already not to want to put them to the test again. As for the archopologist, they might not regard her as so deadly an opponent, but there was no wavering in her stand or unfamiliarity in the way she held her weapon, and none of them was anxious to be the one to discover if she were actually willing to use it.

When the Emirite woman was within easy speaking distance, he motioned her to stop. "Start talking, Cass. I want to know why. You could've done it any time inside. I half expected a hit then, but why now?"

"It wasn't me. Or us. It was him." She jerked her head in the direction of her dead former comrade, not flinching although Murchu's close-range bolt had left little of his face intact. "We didn't even know he was planning to do it."

"A real independent-minded group, aren't you?"

She shrugged. "The son had just dosed on raklik. He'd taken it into his head to hate you, and if his roar went sour, this attack could've been the result. We can't know that for fact, but it stands to reason."

"A raklik user? You people must be voyaging with deprogrammed navputers to set out with one of those."

Once again, the woman shrugged. "You did us a favor."

"We'll let it lie there, then," he said coldly. "Doctor Lis and I want to be about our business. You stay nice and quiet until we're gone, then forget about us and get rid of that debris however you see fit."

* * * *

Neither man nor woman breathed freely until the last vestige of the rough spaceport faded from their sight.

Banna exhaled in a long, wavering sigh and pressed her hands to her eyes. "None of my professors ever mentioned anything like that when lecturing us on situations we might possibly encounter during field expeditions."

"I imagine they wouldn't," Murchu replied grimly. "It is over, though. We're away with it."

"Truly? They will not be after us?"

He nodded. "Truly."

"You believe her, then? About the raklik?"

"The raklik? Of course not. No starship's master, much less a pirate, would dare voyage with a user aboard. If one did sign on, he'd be chained in the hold once he betrayed himself, which he would do in short order, until he could be dumped at the first planetfall." Or dumped in space in the case of raiders.

"That is what I had believed, but—"

"The bastard was in his right mind, twisted as it was—I saw enough of his face to be sure of that—but I do believe he was acting on his own. I'd say he was an all-around misfit, one of those defectives unable to tolerate opposition in any form and probably not particularly receptive to taking orders as well. If so, he wouldn't have lasted much longer in that company. It's a deadly aberration for someone making his living traveling the starlanes, whatever his calling."

"You did not have much time with them," she ventured doubtfully. "If you're wrong, those renegades could be following us even now."

"Power down. They've been told to let us be."

"Told?"

The Ranger-Captain gave her a tight smile. "Aye. Think. This is a big, carefully planned operation. The ones in charge of it would research any planet where they wanted to park their precious hot cargo until they could pick it up themselves. They'd have learned about your work on Ruby and know of your plans to return, probably within the time frame of interest to them. Their bully boys would have been warned about you and given strict orders not to trouble you. Your reputation is such that they'd realize you'd be well monitored and any interference might call down a lot of attention on Ruby of Diamond just when they didn't want any at all, maybe enough to blow their whole plan to stardust."

"So the fact that they did not try to blast us out of space or jump us at once was proof they are the ones we want," she mused thoughtfully.

"It was a strong indication they could be, enough to encourage me to go ahead as I did instead of aborting at once and trying another approach."

"But they did not ignore us," Banna pointed out.

"That could hardly be expected. They had to confirm who you were. They were content to leave you alone once they did. I was a wild card, however. You'd come alone the last time, remember? They didn't anticipate seeing me, and so I required some closer scrutiny. I was able to satisfy most of them, but somehow that Albionan got his hackles up against me from the start."

"Did he suspect you're Patrol, do you think?

"No. If he'd thought I was with the Stellar Patrol, he'd have blurted that out right away. He didn't do it out of my hearing, either, or I'd have had more trouble with the rest of them."

"They might be playing with us or trying to find out how much we know," the Auroran reasoned.

Murchu looked at her with new respect "The sons couldn't take the chance. If they had any suspicion we were government-connected, they'd have eliminated us immediately, orders or not. They've got too much at stake. If a pirate's captured, he's as good as executed. Their bosses' profits or annoyance wouldn't weigh very heavily against that prospect. They'd have to take care of us."

"Maybe they would take care of us," the woman corrected. "The Albionan did not do particularly well when he tried."

Taigue's eyes glittered coldly. "Those chaps are space fighters and damn good in that element. On-world combat, anything beyond gang work, or a blaster-bolt, or knife thrust in a back alley, puts them at a disadvantage. Rangers, on the other hand, are accustomed to managing themselves in a variety of surplanetary situations. That worked to our good this time."

His mouth hardened. "The poor bastard wound up helping us in the end."

There was a tightness in his voice as he said that which made the archopologist look sharply at him. "How so?"

"Raiders are no fools. I handled myself awfully well in the fight for an average space hound. The doubts you're worrying about might well have arisen later but for this."

"I do not understand."

His hands whitened momentarily on the controls. "A Stellar Patrol agent in either branch of the service would have shot out the front wheels and tried to take that man on stun. To just burn him down as I did should have been unthinkable."

Chapter Eight

The off-worlders rode in relative silence for what remained of the afternoon. Both were uncomfortable, although they voiced no complaint against the ever-present chill or their cramped position.

They had quickly put on face masks. The cold was sharp in itself, and the wind generated by even the modest pace they were able to achieve caused it to cut through bare flesh like a giant's knife. Taigue shivered under the worst blasts, but he found himself so absorbed in the desolate yet striking world around them that he could more or less ignore the unpleasantness of the journey for long stretches of time.

They were traveling along the relatively flat bed of an ancient river. The surface was hard, as the archopologist had promised, chiefly packed gravel cut occasionally by lava flows of varying widths.

Cliffs and respectably sized hills could be seen on either bank, some actually forming that bank, other rolling back in what would have been a glorious landscape had Ruby of Diamond been a living planet bright with growing things and the animals they should have sustained.

The man felt an aching inside him as he studied the wasteland around them. Most of these rises were the product of Ruby's dying, sharp, angry extrusions spat up as her heart burned and writhed, but a few had known a different world. Wind and rain and flowing water had worked on them. Roots had pried into their crevices and folds, seeking nourishment and support, before thirst and cold and seismic violence had made an end of them.

His head lowered. How he wished he might have seen that other Ruby, saved a sampling of her seeds, spacelifted breeding populations of her fauna . . .

He sighed and raised his head. That blue-skied planet was gone past recalling, but the mystery she represented remained, providing interest and challenge enough to hold the attention of any Ranger. His kind were explorers, after all, not the second-line Commandos they were so frequently forced to become, and there was much to be discovered here.

He tried to put their present position into perspective in his mind from what he could recall of the maps he had studied. The old waterway, impressive enough on its own, was part of a massive system draining into a great river which had stretched an awesome thirty-six miles across and had flowed over five thousand miles into the largest of Ruby's eight oceans, whose basins were now vast seas of sand and gravel completely overlaying both the lava beds and the endless ice fields they contained.

The hilly country around them rose gradually in the direction they were traveling, first into the remnants of old, naturally weathered mountains and then, abruptly, into a maze of newer peaks. These were equal in size to any thus far discovered in the ultrasystem, and their contorted forms mirrored the ferocity of the forces that had created them.

There was no change in color, no break in the eternal red of the ground and heights, but even that was not entirely a monotony. There were differences in shade, in texture, in the effects of glare and shadow satisfying to an eye willing to seek them out and sensitive enough to appreciate the subtle variations it found.

Taigue shifted himself as much as the crates hemming him in would allow. Every muscle in his body ached from being held in very nearly this one position for all these hours, and despite his Arctic gear, he was becoming increasingly more aware of the cold. He tried to turn his thoughts back to their former train, but he could no longer ignore the rapidly dropping temperature.

He dared not do so. It was well below zero, although Diamond had not yet slipped beneath the horizon. Well clad as they were, they were still in danger of taking cold damage, particularly in their nearly immobilized extremities. Already the pain in his feet was becoming an agony despite his flexing and stamping them constantly to keep the circulation going in them.

The Ranger-Captain looked at Banna, who was nearing the end of her shift as driver. Her fingers were extending and closing in a futile effort to force the chill and numbness out of them as they grasped the controls.

"We'll either have to stop outright or take turns walking. Otherwise, we'll both be badly frostbitten before much longer," he told her.

"We shall stop," she replied decisively. "We could not make the dig before full dark anyway, not after that delay in port, and I do not fancy traveling on without light. –One spot is as good as the next?"

"Aye, though we should remain on this level. We have more shelter from the wind down here than we would on the bank even if we could drag the flier up there."

* * * *

It was a relief just to be out of the machine and moving again. That and the prospect of gaining some degree of comfort lent speed to their actions, and it was not long before they had their tent raised and secured, and the miniature stove in operation.

The Auroran fastened the entrance flap and returned to the central part of the shelter, almost whimpering in her relief at feeling the warmth already radiating from the efficient heater.

These were not luxury quarters. The dome-shaped tent was purely a survival tool. It was small, barely large enough to accommodate the stove and their two sleeping bags. It was also quite low, only high enough at its center to permit them to sit upright. In its favor, it was well insulated, and little of the heat generated within it escaped into the frigid outer world. No light would pass beyond it, either, and they would be able to rest secure knowing it would not act as a beacon to draw anyone out searching the night for them.

Murchu already had their supper cooking. He was taking advantage of the stove rather than merely quick-frying the rations on his plutonium disk. Hungry as she was, Lis was glad of that. This was a slower method, but it resulted in a tastier meal.

She was tired enough to let him at it, too tired really for one who had spent the last several hours sitting, whatever the lack of comfort. The tension and fear of the day were getting to her more than its labors.

Banna ate quickly when the food was done, as did her companion. Neither of them said much while busy with their food or later. Each was absorbed in his own thoughts, and it was apparent to her that weariness was working on the man as strongly as it was on her.

She studied Taigue speculatively from beneath half-closed lids. He had the courtesy not to try to conceal how tired he was, but there was more than that riding him. His face was drawn and haggard. His eyes, which, unlike hers, were fully open, looked into some dark distance invisible to her.

She wished she could do something to help him.

Determination firmed within her. She jolly well had better do something. No man should be left to face hell alone.

The archopologist slid across the three feet separating them. Her hand gently closed over his. "Taigue?" He looked at her. He seemed surprised by her intrusion but not to resent it, and her grasp tightened a little. "It is still bothering you, what happened back at the port?"

"Aye, it bothers me. It's a whole lot easier to kill a starship. We can make ourselves forget there's a crew aboard." The Ranger-Captain freed his hand and drew away from her. "Expediency over life. Maybe we agents merit the name of butcher some people want to tack on us."

"No, you do not." She glared at him. "You sound like a certified vacuum brain. —I saw it, Taigue. You are a fighter, like it or not, and your instinct took command. What would blowing out the front one or two wheels have accomplished when all the son had to do was take to the air? Even if you did stop the vehicle, you would not have had time to take down the driver as well. As for stunning him, I know a little about a blaster's power. You could not have been sure of winning through the windshield at that setting. You did precisely what the conditions of the battle demanded of you."

Rather than argue with her, Taige scowled as he stared at his empty plate.

The Auroran glared at her companion. "What would you have done had you made him your prisoner? Turned him over to the invisible on-world Patrol agents we somehow wished into existence? Waited with him until the Regulars could be summoned from Sapphire? His comrades knew you recognized what they are. You could not simply have handed him over to them with the request that they deliver him to the authorities even though you could be fairly certain they would burn him down themselves the moment we vanished over the horizon."

Murchu nodded slowly, but then his shoulders fell, and he shook his head. "It's not just that," he told her dully. "The killing back there might be the most dramatic instance, but it sure as all the Federation's hells wasn't the first time I've stepped beyond prescribed procedure. The nonsense I pulled on you back on Aurora is graphic proof of that."

Banna's eyes dropped. His fear was real and not groundless. This man carried a great deal of responsibility as a front-line officer in a hard-pressed organization. Any aberration on his part could have serious ramifications well beyond his own person and beyond the Stellar Patrol as well.

For a moment, she felt paralyzed. She did not know him or his history well enough to dismiss this black doubt of himself outright, and false comfort would be less than useless.

Her instincts had rarely played her false, and she had what she had seen to back her words. "You are not a butcher," Banna Lis told him firmly, "and whatever liberties you may have taken with its rules of conduct on occasion, you are a credit to your service. If you do sense a bent in yourself which you see as potentially dangerous, that is another matter entirely. It is up to you to put chains on it and keep them fast. As for the fight today," she continued practically, "it was ugly for a fact, but I much prefer it was that space jackal who died and not one of us."

The gray eyes studied her somberly. It was difficult to accept this attitude as genuine in a woman of the inner systems, and one of their intellectuals at that. "I hope my superiors see it the way you do," he told her mildly.

"Your superiors?"

"An agent has to account for mortalities occurring during his assignments, Banna." His mouth hardened. "We can't just be allowed to go sowing corpses throughout the ultrasystem."

"You are not required to let yourselves be slaughtered, are you?"

"Naturally not."

"Then you should have nothing to worry about, especially since you were responsible for a civilian as well as for your own life."

The Auroran was quiet a moment. "A check on you service peoples' activities is necessary," she conceded. "Without control in so large a force, some tragedy would almost inevitably occur. It would require

65

only one corrupt or misled agent." The black eyes caught his. "It would not come at your hand. You are far too conscious of the danger to be drawn into it."

There was no mistaking the strength or reality of her assurance. "You're so certain?" he asked. "You haven't known me long, and some of what you've seen isn't entirely to my credit."

She smiled. "I have surprisingly little to lay against you."

Lis was grave again in the next instant. "I have to be able to judge people, friend. The only kind of hands we scientists can get on a great many of our expeditions, especially those taking us to the more out-of-the-way places in the ultrasystem, are either students or people with good reason for being willing to bury themselves somewhere for a while. If I choose wrong, I might not only see my work lost or deliberately destroyed but lose my life and perhaps the lives of others as well."

The Ranger made no response as he regarded her with new perception. He and his colleagues tended to forget that scientists like this woman, searchers after knowledge in a multitude of related and unrelated fields, faced dangers and hardships as part of their daily work that were the equal of any but the most extreme trials afflicting his kind, and they frequently bore them with less protest. He would do well to remember it the next time he was ordered to escort some such party or to check on their progress during a patrol.

Banna Lis was entitled to something more than silence from him. She had cared enough to probe the trouble she had sensed on him, and her strongly expressed confidence had somehow indeed helped. "I owe you for this one," he said slowly. "We're both spent, and I had no business shifting my cargo on you, but I do appreciate your ear."

The Auroran's smile was soft. "We all need a little of that now and then. I suppose we bone diggers tend to be fair listeners. We are forced to be entirely alone so much that we know the value of companionship when we do get to experience it."

The man felt suddenly embarrassed. He straightened. "We'll each have to be alone for the remainder of the night, unfortunately. It would not be wise to abandon guard duty."

He sighed inwardly. He hated the thought of leaving the tent again. The warmth was wonderful, and his sleeping bag seemed like a preview of paradise, but it would be stark madness to ignore the potential for danger, whatever his earlier assurance to his companion.

The archopologist reached for her gloves. "The first turn is mine. – No arguing. I trust you with my life and the welfare of the Federation, Captain, but not that you would not turn gallant and allow me to sleep the night through."

"Would that be so bad?"

"I want you in good shape tomorrow, Taigue Murchu. I do not know how much work I shall be able to knock out of you over the next several weeks, but sure as space is black, you will help me unload and store all this gear." She laughed at his scowl. "We are both equally tired, so there is no real reason not to let me choose my turn."

"Perhaps it is you who'll turn gallant," he countered.

"Not a meteor's chance. I am a mere civilian, after all, utterly incapable of keeping my eyes open a moment longer than my assigned time."

"Aye, and I'm a merchant prince from Hedon." He nodded, smiling. "Very well, Doctor. I surrender. Just make full sure you do wake me, or I warn you, you'll get nothing at all in the way of physical labor out of me."

Chapter Nine

Banna Lis groaned as the insistent beep of her timer jarred through the fog of sleep enveloping her and forced her back into the waking world. It was warm inside her sleeping bag, and she did not want to leave it to face another day of that wretched cold.

Knowing there was no help for it, she steeled herself and released the bag's fastenings. She shivered at the touch of the cooler air which struck her as soon as she threw the covering aside. It could be no more than fifty degrees in the tent, she thought miserably, and even that set her teeth chattering. How was she going to manage during the long hours ahead?

Manage she must, and so Banna hastened about her business. She ate quickly, leftovers from their super of the previous evening, and re-packed her sleeping bag, mess kit, and the few other personal items she had used during the camp period. That done, she pulled on her outer gear and reluctantly opened the little shelter's carefully sealed entrance.

The morning was crystal clear and bitterly cold. The woman forced herself to ignore the last and set about looking for her companion.

She spotted him in the next moment. Murchu was sitting hunched down in the flier, using the bulk of its baggage to keep some of the wind, which was considerably sharper today, off himself. He looked tired and utterly discontented, but she was pleased to see he was fully alert to his surroundings. It was a fine thing for a man to have confidence in his theories, but not if he ignored sensible caution. She was glad to know she was not stuck in this frigid desert with a microwit.

Taigue saw Banna as soon as she emerged and waved his hand in greeting even as he hurried to join her.

"How did your watch go?" she asked.

"Quietly, as expected."

Once he had ascertained the archopologist had eaten, the Ranger began dismantling the tent, leaving the rest of the camp-breaking chores to her. He worked quickly, and by the time Lis had completed the repacking and securing of the flier, he was done.

The brisk work had temporarily warmed him, and it was regret that he stowed their shelter away. "Deserts are supposed to be hot," he grumbled.

"Not all of them," Banna replied calmly. "Besides, I imagine we would be even unhappier in one of those others."

"We would. I know. I've had the misfortune of serving in such territory on more than one occasion."

The woman's eyes sparkled, although she managed to restrain the urge to laugh. "You do not like cold, and you do not like heat. What does please you, Captain Murchu?"

Taigue smiled. "Paradise weather, of course. I never seem to get assigned any place offering such a climate, unfortunately."

His gray eyes watched her somberly as he opened the flier door for her, that on the passenger's side this time, since the driver's slot fell to him. "To be serious for a moment, Banna, are you going to have to put up with conditions like this for the duration?"

"Space, no! Do you imagine I am some sort of ultrawoman? Oh, life will be anything but ideal, and there will be times when I shall have to work completely exposed for fairly extended periods, but on the whole, I shall be inside with a stove going full blast to keep things quite bearable. Sure, even this journey would have been no trouble for us had we left most of our gear back at the spaceport like I usually do and could keep the canopy closed. The flier is adapted for Arctic use, after all, and Ruby's equator is not so much as a challenge for its heating system. The temperature around here at this time of year rises to a balmy ten degrees or so by early afternoon."

"Only a step or two below tropical," he declared sarcastically.

"What made you think I could stand this sort of thing long term?" she asked him curiously. "I know full well that the last impression I give is of possessing uncommon hardiness or having any love at all of personal discomfort."

"No, but the acquisition of knowledge can be as addictive as anything else, quite as binding in its way as the chains raklik sets on its habitual users. It can override most other considerations. I personally brought down a once-highly-respected man who had murdered his supervisor because she had refused him access to some sensitive data he wanted for a study he was conducting purely to satisfy his personal curiosity. No concrete gain whatsoever would have resulted from it."

"You do not imagine me repeating that?" the woman demanded hotly.

"I can't envision anything possessing you to such an extent." In truth, he could not imagine her possessed by any force or passion. "But the need to know is there, and you love your job, Banna. You're not merely good at it. That kind of motivation can steel an individual to endure a great deal."

"A great deal, yes, but not to the point of suicide, which is the practical equivalent to failing to take proper precautions against Ruby of Diamond's weather and other deficiencies. I assure you, I am not scramble-circuited enough to risk that, or to forego any more comfort than I absolutely must, either."

No, he thought, but his own experience told him something of what she had to put up with on most such expeditions, however much she might choose to minimize that aspect of her life. This brand of courage was one he readily understood and respected.

It was more than respect that he felt for Banna Lis of Aurora. Tenderness filled him. With the whole of his being, he wanted to shield her from everything threatening her. At the same time, he recognized this was not a woman who could be sheltered in such a manner. She had chosen a demanding lifeway with full knowledge of the charter she was taking on, and her choice had to be respected. To do otherwise was a denial and rejection of Banna herself.

The Ranger-Captain sighed and turned his thoughts from his companion to the place in which they found themselves.

The stark countryside flowing by them—or above them in the increasingly more frequent places where the banks retained their full height despite the chaos which had torn this part of the planet since water had last flowed between them—grew perceptibly more rugged, the rises higher and sharper, with each mile they passed. An increasing number of the latter were old formations, born in Ruby's life rather than in her death.

It was among such cliffs that the ruins they were seeking were located, and he began to speculate about them and to wonder about the lost race who had built them.

By all accounts, those long-dead people had raised no insignificant monuments to themselves, although they had apparently possessed only a very limited armory of tools from what could be deduced from the structures they had created.

That evidence told extremely little about the vanished on-worlders save they had unquestionably been accomplished. Even the nature of their possessions and the kind of knowledge they had held and valued would probably never be known, not unless new and incalculably richer finds were made and studied by scientists like Banna Lis. As for the known sites, there were only three, all nearly barren of artifacts, but they were impressive in themselves and told of a once-heavy population united in a well-organized society and, later, of their tenacity and marvelous adaptability.

None of that had availed them in the end, of course. The catastrophe striking down Ruby of Diamond had been too appalling, too overwhelming in its scope, for any isolated prespace populace to overcome.

He thought of them in their last, desperate, doomed struggle to survive, and though he did not know what they had looked like or whether they had been human at all, his heart ached for and with them, as if he were one of their own. He longed to know them, to learn whatever time and a planet's death throws had left for discovery.

Taigue Murchu had read the Auroran's published reports, but now he began to probe her for greater detail and for the impressions she herself had received from the sites, the theories she had formed during her studies of them but had not yet released for one reason or another.

Banna was pleasantly surprised by his questions, which showed considerable depth of thought and bore little direct relation to his assignment, but she answered them as fully as she could, quickly warming to her subject as he proved himself to be a receptive and intelligent audience.

The better part of three hours thus passed very agreeably despite the numbing temperature, but at the end of that time, they brought the flier to a stop before one of the now rare spots where some force or other, in this case a lava flow, had raised the river bed until it was almost level with the bank.

"If we can get up there and cut across country, we will chop a good ten miles off our journey. The river ran an extremely convoluted course along all this next stretch."

The man looked at the place critically, then at their overburdened machine. "We should be able to do it," he announced decisively. "There are only a few feet to climb, and it's really more a slope than a sheer wall. We'll have a go at it at any rate."

It would have been a simple task had they been able to get the vehicle even a few inches off the ground, but it would not lift at all though they both came out to lighten it.

"We shall have to unload it," the archopologist said with a sigh.

"Too much work. I'll try to drive it up first, before we resort to that."

Banna glanced at the slope doubtfully but started for the flier. "If you think you can do it, I am game."

"No, you stay back. There'll be that much less weight in it." And that much less to risk if he succeeded only in crashing the bloody thing.

Taigue started the engine, reversing first to give himself something of a run, then opened the throttle to the full.

The vehicle lumbered toward the wall. The Ranger's heart slammed hard in his breast. Would it have lift enough to follow the slope even though it could not actually leave the ground, or would it slam into the wall? If it could not climb and struck that squarely at this pace . . .

The flier hit, bounced, and started to ascend.

It advanced steadily for about thirty inches, but the force driving it was not sufficient to maintain its rise. He felt the machine stop and then begin to lose ground despite its engine's fight to push it ahead.

In desperation, Murchu activated the flight mechanism. The vehicle made a jerking leap in response to the sudden upsurge of power, actually leaving the ground for an almost immeasurably brief instant.

It came down again with a bone-jarring thud and a fierce grinding of gears. The man fought the controls for the next several fraction-seconds while the flier bucked and swerved like an untamed living thing, knowing he was dead and their transportation a wreck if it tore back down onto the dry bed now.

Finally, after a brief seeming eternity, it met no resistance save that of the air and straightened. He brought it to a stop on the level bank.

His eyes closed but opened again in the next instant. The Ranger looked around him in satisfaction. He was up, where he wanted to be, and a safe eighteen inches at the nearest point from the rim. It had been a chancy performance, he thought grimly, however successful. Too chancy. He had been a shooting star to go on with it, but at least it had ended well.

Banna, with only her own nimble body to concern her, scrambled up without difficulty. "That was stellar-class driving, Taigue," she called out to him as soon as she regained her feet. "I do not know of anyone else who could have pulled it off."

Murchu gave her a salute as smart as any Regular's. "Just part of the service, Doctor. Hop in."

He cringed visibly as a blast of wind struck him, its icy claws cutting through his garments to tear his shivering flesh like knives. He had realized they had been receiving good shelter in the river bed but had underestimated how bad full exposure would prove.

The archopologist turned her masked face away from it and so hunched her shoulders that she seemed to literally draw in upon herself.

She straightened as soon as the gust's force was spent. "I had not guessed how dreadful this would be without proper shelter. If you find it too rough, we can go back down."

Taigue barely bit back his furious retort in time. Banna had not been striking at his hardihood but rather had been deferring to his greater experience. She was willing to go on, to endure this ordeal in order to end their journey that much sooner, but if he believed their danger would be significantly increased by doing so, she would bow to his judgment.

"After going through all that?" he managed to demand lightly. "Not a meteor's chance, Doctor Lis. We continue on from here."

Chapter Ten

Many a time during the following two hours, Taigue Murchu bitterly regretted those words, but pride and also sense held him to the course they had chosen. He would not be the one to beg for a retreat, not while this civilian woman could bear the same punishment in silence. Besides, they had been miserable on their old route as well. Since their peril was not very much greater, their best move all around was to conclude the journey as quickly as possible.

Driving was challenging over this more broken terrain. The ground itself was rugged, strewn with obstacles and breaks, and the flier had never been designed for such travel. Although a rough-country vehicle meant to be versatile, its wheels had still been intended for short-term use over gentler land, and there was always the danger of its tipping over or suffering some damage irreparable by the tools they had on hand.

It was only when Banna took over the controls once more that he had any leisure to devote his thoughts once more to Ruby herself and the grim fate she had suffered.

What had this place been like then? Had there been forests or more widely spaced woodlands or rolling grasslands here? Perhaps some or all of it had been cultivated land. The ruins which were their destination had been a fairly populous community, and it was not impossible that at least the peripherals of the territory supporting it had spread out this far.

He sighed to himself. Now nothing remained, not even a line of ancient ditches or the skeletons of trees to tell what had once been. Ruby of Diamond was so dead, so arid and so cold, that her very ghosts had perished.

A long, undulating bellow rose out of the desert in front of them, and the Ranger gasped. "What in the name of space was that?" His blaster was already in his hand..

"I . . . do not know," the equally startled woman replied.

Before either of them could speak again, the call came a second time.

The Auroran's head cocked to one side. "It might be a cam, Taigue. They are not noisy beasts normally, but if something gives them cause, they can get quite loud. I have never heard a sound like that from them, though. I fear I am no expert," she concluded apologetically.

"You probably never encountered one in real difficulty. I know less than you do about cams, but I can usually recognize a creature in trouble when I hear one. –Come on. He's not far away."

As if in response, the invisible animal bellowed again.

Taking a fix from the sound, the pair soon located the source a scant hundred yards from the place where they had first heard it, concealed by one of the many low, sharp ridges so prevalent in the region.

He was fastened there. The animal, a bull of the species, jerked his head and moved a few steps in their direction, but the chain leading from his halter and looped over the slender stone spire to which it was fastened held him firmly in place.

The archopologist spat out a spacer's expletive and leaped from the flier. "The bastards!" she snarled. "Look, he is lame. When he either could not keep pace or refused what probably was an immoderate load in the first place, those thrice-accursed sons of Schythian apes just tied him up here and left him to die. They did not even give him the chance to follow after them as best he could or to return to the spaceport." Her brows creased in a distressed frown. "It is an unusually cruel doom for such a gregarious creature. Cams love and will always seek the company of their own kind and especially their mates, with whom they are bonded for life. –They need that contact, damn it. According to the handlers I met, it is a real torment for them to be in isolation for any length of time."

Murchu studied the big creature. His heritage was obvious, although the differences between the cam and the parent stock from which he had sprung were more striking than were the similarities.

The bull was fully as tall as he was long. A poor retention, that last, Tigue thought. It was helpful to a beast in a hot environment where the air even a few feet off the ground could be many degrees cooler than on the baked soil, but in the cold, it gave greater play to the wind.

Apart from that, he was well adapted to the harsh life of tundra and steppe.

No single or double hump rode the straight back. Instead, the cam carried his very heavy fat reserves evenly spread over his barrel-shaped trunk and the short neck so different from that of his Terran ancestors. The head and nose and the supple, leathery lips and tongue were basically identical to those of the original animal, as were the huge, cushioned hooves meant to carry him over hard surfaces or soft sand or snow alike.

Mutation had given him a coat superbly fitted to combat low temperatures. The whole body, including the otherwise standard head and nose, was covered by heavy, long, dark-brown hair. Beneath that grew a second layer, not hair this time but soft, curling wool so thick a man could scarcely force his fingers through it to touch the skin it guarded, thus keeping out the wind and holding the bulk of the heat the animal generated close to its own body. The same thick blanket screened the long legs, and a particular variation of it formed the water-repelling hoof padding which shielded the big feet from both burning sands and the bitter, penetrating bite of ice.

The greater part of Ruby of Diamond was beyond their powers of endurance, but their formidable insulation should not only keep cams alive but quite comfortable in tundra conditions far more severe than were to be found here on the dead planet's equator.

Taigue did not know more about the animals than Banna had told him earlier, but the bull appeared to be in basically good shape despite his ordeal apart from having a very lame right hind leg. The trouble was in the foot, the hoof, he decided after a few minutes' observation, basing his diagnosis on the manner in which the cam held it raised a few inches off the ground and the way he strove to put as little weight as possible on it when he moved.

As he drew closer, Murchu noticed several small red spots glinting on the chain, and his anger rose to match his companion's. Blood. Flecks of frozen blood left when the poor thing had tried to chew his way through the cold, unyielding metal.

The man held his rage in check. A Stellar Patrol agent met with cruelty all too often in the course of his work and learned to maintain his control in the face of it. More could generally be accomplished by a cool mind than by an overwrought one.

"How long do you think he's been here?" he asked.

"A week maybe. The ones I saw before were much rounder. They draw on their fat when they must go without drink and food even as their parent stock do." She gave the bull a pitying look. "That is really just a guess about the time. I do not know enough about them to judge an individual's weight loss accurately, and I . . . I have never seen one that has been abused before."

There was a break in her voice as she said the last. Aurorans could not abide the mistreatment of any creature. That was why they had become such implacable fighters once they had been made acquainted with the realities of Arcturian occupation, whatever the initial reluctance of most of them to enlist as active participants in the war effort.

"A few days more or less probably doesn't matter," Taigue assured her. "He doesn't seem to have suffered much real damage. How long can they go without water?"

"Any water? A month or so, and even a little light dew will extend that period considerably. A cam can drop more than a third of its body weight without taking harm. Eventually, though, once their fat has been leached dry, they suffer the same fate as the rest of us." Her expression darkened. "Poor fellow. He must be frightfully thirsty all the same. Cams are not happy in an extended drought, however well they can endure it."

"His unhappiness saved this one. It was his smelling us, or our water more likely, that caused him to bellow the way he did. He's quiet now, you notice."

The woman's shoulders straightened. "Well, he shall have satisfaction from us. —Fetch one of the water tanks and bring it here. While he is slacking his thirst, we can set about freeing him and see what we can do for his leg." A thought struck her. "You do know something about tending to animals?"

"A bit. Unfortunately, not a great deal about domestic ones."

"Good. Everything will help. I can treat humans for basic injuries and the like, but I would not know where to begin with him." She jerked her head in the direction of the flier. "Fetch the first aid kit and see what you can do," she told him, addressing him as she would a grunt laborer in her distraction over their patient.

"Aye." Murchu turned on his heel and stalked toward the flier.

The Auroran's eyes narrowed slightly as she watched him go. That one was an officer to the core. He did not like taking orders, not from a civilian at any rate.

She shrugged in her mind. It was his problem, not hers. It had been his idea to accompany her as an expedition hand, and until his real work called him away, she had every right and every intention of utilizing him in that capacity. She had not been given much choice or consideration when it came to accepting his company after all.

Banna immediately felt ashamed of her thoughts. Taigue Murchu was a good man. If he bore a full complement of human failings, that was only to be accepted as the lot of all their species. None of his flaws were base or potentially dangerous as far as she could see, and his strengths far outweighed them

She watched him struggle with one of the self-heated tanks which held their water and kept it from freezing. Her eyes softened. Taigue was kind, and his years of too-close acquaintance with the darker ways of their species had not stripped him of his basic sense of justice. She had seen the anger ripple through him at the sight of the cam's plight. He had kept it in check rather than giving vent to it as she had, but she liked him the better for that. She preferred dealing with a man in good command of himself.

Murchu's work necessitated self-control. His work. The thought of that excited her, particularly those tasks the Exploratory Force had been created to perform. Rangers explored planets and assisted the Settlement Board and the scientific teams studying them. Occasionally, they discovered worlds and were privileged to make the initial contact with previously unknown peoples. They had space, the stars, and they had the thrill of visiting and actually knowing some of the ultrasystem's most unique planets. It was a calling to be envied by anyone possessing her brand of curiosity, the need to know as he himself had named it, anyone willing to accept the hardship and inevitable perils inherent in the challenging of the unknown.

Their newer, more unwelcome duties were no less worthy. Rangers of the Exploratory Force did carry on a war of sorts, fiercer, deadlier in one sense than that being waged by the two great ultrasystems. The soldiers of the Arcturian Empire were at least honorable men for the vastly greater part. Those against whom the Stellar Patrol fought could also handle their weapons well, but they were the dregs of their system, the vicious vermin who would parasitize the Federation to its death if left to flourish unchecked. In the course of that endless undeclared war, Rangers often carried out missions which would have won the admiration of the rightly famed Commandos. Through it all, they, like their Regular counterparts in space, battled on knowing they would never receive a fraction of the respect or support the military enjoyed, that they would often have to function under the distrust and occasionally the open opposition of the citizens they were striving to protect. They fought because it was necessary that they do so. Scant wonder they sometimes felt small trust in and even less liking for those not of their service.

Well, she, for one, respected them in full. She respected Ranger-Captain Taigue Murchu, and she liked him. He was a solid friend, and were conditions right, he could be something more than a friend.

The woman sighed then. There was no forgetting he was a Terran, in his concepts if not actually by birth. The most of them were so damnably conscious of prototype . . .

She shook her head, dismissing her momentary fancy. There was more to occupy her mind right now than her companion's personal ideal of physical perfection.

Chapter Eleven

The Ranger-Captain was sweating despite the cold by the time he had finished lugging the clumsy container to the waiting archopologist.

"You asked for this," he grunted accusingly as he stood it upright before her.

Banna Lis had to fight herself not to smile. He sounded as if he would murder her if she said one of the lighter tanks would have done as well. "That, I did, friend. Let us get the top off and treat our foundling to a proper drink. He deserves one, I think, after waiting so patiently for us to get around to helping him."

No sooner had Taigue complied than the cam rammed his nose into the liquid and began sucking it up eagerly in tremendous, nearly continuous gulps.

Murchu frowned in concern as he watched the level of water in the big container drop. "Can we afford this, Banna?"

"Oh, yes. I can claim recompense in kind from the Settlement Board for any supplies I use in caring for their property."

"Repayment might take a while to get here," he pointed out. "We could be good and thirsty before any replacements reach us."

"Are you suggesting we let the beast go dry?" she demanded sharply.

"Not at all," the man replied calmly. "He needs this dose, but we should consider rationing him from now on, or none of us may have anything left to drink.

Banna felt more relieved than she would have imagined. "Have some confidence in me, Captain. I have worked on Ruby before, and you may believe me when I say potential lack of water is one of the least of our concerns."

"That says some bad things about our greater concerns," he muttered dourly.

She laughed. "Trust me, Taigue Murchu. I shall explain later, but right now, this poor creature does need medical attention."

"Very well. Hold him by the halter. Keep his head steady so he'll feel controlled. I don't fancy a clip from one of those hooves."

"I will try."

Lis approached the bull steadily, her movements smooth and quiet, and cautiously reached for his halter. These mutant animals were better tempered than the creatures from which they had sprung, but she knew from experience that they had retained the originals' penchant for spitting, if anything with an improvement in their already decidedly too accurate aim.

Taigue grasped the injured foot firmly. He was no stockman, but training and natural interest had given him a basic working knowledge of the more common types of animals found throughout the Federation and some skill in handling and caring for those most frequently associating with humans in one capacity or another. That knowledge could be applied here.

He did not have to struggle to lift the hoof or keep it raised, at least—the cam had no desire whatsoever to lower it—and there was excellent light so he was able to get a good look at it.

A good look at the matted hair covering the hard outer hoof and the cushion where the problem probably lay, he amended mentally. What was he to do? If he cut the mass away or even trimmed it, he would be depriving the animal of his first defense against this frozen, rugged land, maybe dooming him to a worse state than the one in which he presently was.

He stripped off his gloves and lay them on the discarded cover of the water tank. Working gently but persistently, he probed with his fingers, pushing them through the hair in search of signs of heating or swelling or of a foreign body. Old, clotted blood made his task more difficult still but told him he was on the right track. The fact that it had remained unfrozen to dry like this gave testimony to the efficiency of the cam's natural defenses and confirmed the correctness of his decision to proceed in this manner instead of taking the easier course of shaving the hoof.

The search took several minutes, minutes which seemed like hours to the two humans as they stood open to the buffeting of the sharp wind, but at last, he touched something. "I have it, I think," he hissed, purposely keeping his voice low and free of excitement lest he startle his patient. "This hair's remarkable," he added appreciatively despite the trouble it was giving him. "By rights, my fingers should be too numb by now to feel anything at all."

"What is it?" Banna demanded curiously.

"A stone, I believe. A sharp, thin sliver. It went in on an angle, and every step drove it deeper."

"An unfortunate accident."

"It probably got him at just the wrong moment and point." His voice hardened. "This wouldn't have amounted to much if those bastards had taken a few minutes to dig it out when he first picked it up. Now it's really embedded, and pulling it free is going to be a stellar-class job."

"But you can do it?" the woman asked anxiously.

"I'm going to try."

The Ranger released the cam's leg long enough to remove a bottle and a forceps from the first aid kit he had lugged with him along with the water tank. The anesthetic was not terribly powerful, but it was penetrating, and it took effect quickly. If he could get it down to the injury, it should numb the area sufficiently to permit him to remove the offending stone and sterilize the wound after probing it for additional foreign matter.

Carefully parting the hair again, only a slightly easier task this time, he irrigated the wound. After waiting several seconds for the nerve-deadening chemical to take effect, he moved in with the forceps. Although he knew where the sliver was located, it was deep, and he had trouble getting a stolid grip on it.

Once his instrument held it steadily, he was able to apply firm pressure on it, and the stone came out fairly easily.

Taigue gave an open sigh of relief. Had the sliver been notched so that it held itself in the cam's flesh, he would have been forced to cut it out, creating a major wound instead of this thin slice which minor treatment and a protective general anti-infective shot would settle.

Cleansing and dressing the hoof took only a few minutes longer.

He sealed the forceps in one of the bags provided for the purpose and returned it to the kit, where it would remain thus safeguarded from contaminating anything stored with it until he got around to sterilizing it again.

Murchu was smiling when he turned to his companion. "That went a galaxy better than it might have," he declared with satisfaction.

"G-good."

He looked swiftly at her. The woman had steadfastly held to her post, but she was hunched up and was shivering so violently under the cruel lashing of the wind that the tremors rending her were clearly visible despite her bulky clothing.

Taigue hastened to put himself between her and the worst gusts, taking care not to make the service obvious. He did not imagine Banna Lis would much care for favors that pointed up her weakness while the man with her was suffering in equal measure.

Actually, he was suffering more sharply, but he had no call to whine because of that. He had brought it on himself when he had allowed his irritation to goad him into working up a sweat while dragging that blasted tank to the bull instead of taking his time with the job. Now the moisture was clinging to him, drawing the cold and increasing the virulence of its bite until he could have moaned aloud in his distress.

That, he would not do while any will remained to him, but he was certain, had he not been masked, his face would have betrayed the full measure of his misery.

He made no mention of their discomfort but only told the archopologist to unfasten the cam while he restored what was left of the water to the flier. The end loop of the chain had just been dropped over the stone and would present no problem to her.

When he was ready, he returned to her and joined the Auroran in studying their foundling intently.

The cam seemed no worse for wear. He looked contented after his long drink, and between the anesthetic and the relief brought by the removal of the physical irritant, he was standing firmly on the injured leg.

"Will he be able to travel, Taigue?" Banna asked. "He was terribly lame."

"He should if we take it easy." He grimaced. "The pace we're keeping wouldn't cause problems even if he had two legs out instead of just one."

Chapter Twelve

The Ranger-Captain gave a surreptitious, anxious glance at his companion. The cold was beating her down. She scarcely spoke now save when necessary, reserving her strength and will to battle the inescapable enemy clawing at her. He could all but see her face behind its mask, her fine features set in her determination to endure, and he ached to do something, anything, to ease the journey for her.

He was powerless to help either her or himself. His ice gray eyes flickered to the temperature gage. It was 1300 hours now, and the day was about as warm as it was going to get, many degrees warmer than it had been when they had rescued the cam. That did not help. Nothing did. The wind was too high for them to gain any relief in their exposed situation. The flier's heater kept their feet from freezing. The sleeping bags wrapped around them prevented hypothermia. They were safe enough. He had been able to see to that, but there was nothing he could do for their comfort.

The journey itself had grown interminable. They seemed to be barely creeping along. Once the anesthetic had worn off, they had been forced to slow their already inadequate pace still further to accommodate the limping animal, but he could not rightly so much as claim the dubious satisfaction of cursing the beast for delaying them. They would have been forced to drop speed in any case because of the increasing roughness of the terrain. There was just so much challenge the abused flier could be expected to take.

As for the bull, apart from his tender hoof, he appeared to be faring better than either of his two rescuers as he plodded along tirelessly behind them, seemingly untroubled by the low temperature and high wind.

Murchu shifted position slightly. How much longer before they reached their destination?

There was more than impatience behind that mental question. If the remaining distance was too long, he would have to order an early halt. They were weakening, both of them, and he could not permit that deterioration to continue indefinitely, or they would be in real trouble. Part of him welcomed such a break and a return to the relative comfort of the tent, but his very heart quailed at the thought of enduring another such day or part of a day.

Even as he turned to ask her opinion, Banna Lis straightened. "We are almost home," she told him with undisguised relief. "See that cliff ahead of us, close by the river?"

"Aye. The ruins are there?"

"Not in that one. In a ridge just behind it."

"Let's go, Doctor. We won't get there soon enough for me."

"I know." The Auroran sighed. "We should have gone back to the river bed when we discovered what it was like up here with no canopy to shield us."

"The difference was merely one of degree. We would've enjoyed the journey no more." He smiled. "And we wouldn't have found our stray cam, either."

"No," she replied seriously. "It's worth a chilling to have been able to help him."

* * * *

Neither of the off-worlders was as conscious of the numbing cold with the end of their ordeal all but at hand, and before much more time had passed, the ancient structure which was their goal loomed before them.

Taigue Murchu stared at it in frank awe. He had read Banna's reports and had listened to her descriptions, but none of that had prepared him for the actual sight of it.

It was tall, five stories in all, and was fashioned of stone blocks, each almost the twin of the next and so perfectly dressed and fitted that the whole presented a unified, smooth face to the desolate world around it. Although he knew the bulk of the structure had been cut out of the ridge itself rather than manually assembled and raised, this was still an astonishing feat for a primitive people to have accomplished.

"A stone-age race built this?" he asked incredulously more of himself than of his companion.

"Only in the sense that stone tools were used to construct it. There is no question the society responsible for this complex had progressed well beyond the hunter-gatherer level. It merely advanced on a different schedule from that followed by Terrans and had not yet mastered the mining and working of metals on any significant scale."

"You're sure about that?" Such a basic lacking seemed inconceivable to him in the face of the building before him, the more especially given the abundance of iron on Ruby of Diamond.

The archopologist read his last doubt easily enough. It was one she had considered herself.

"Metal trapped in the richest ore is of little value to those lacking the knowledge of how to extract it," she pointed out. "I can speak fairly certainly about the construction methods used here. The marks, the scars if you will, on these blocks, and the manner in with they were dressed, testify that which they were dressed testify that they were worked with stone. The patterns are consistent wherever they are created and are readily apparent throughout this project.

"Do not think less of the Rubians because they had no better. The rest of their techniques were more sophisticated. Even the little evidence we possess shows they had pulleys and tackle, and we feel pretty certain that they used levers as well. Space only knows what else they could do which left no sign for us to read."

He smiled. "So you have said before, Doctor. –What's it like inside?" He had heard her describe this place several times, but now, facing the magnificent ruin, he wanted to hear it all again despite the cold and his former eagerness to escape out of it.

Banna shared his feeling of awe for the ancient structure, and her voice was soft when she responded. She did not lecture but rather recalled the information in her own mind as much for herself as for him.

"The upper four floors contain what I have termed flats, since each appears to have housed a single, relatively small family or other similar group. They are all alike, a central room where the fire was located and three or, more commonly, four chambers leading off from it. Those are more large niches cut out of the wall than true rooms. All the smaller units are on the topmost story."

"Those lines of round indentations are the windows?"

"Yes. They are funnel-shaped, and the openings inside are considerably larger, but only a little light is admitted even when they are left open. The interiors must always have been dark and quite smoky as well."

Her eyes ran along the startlingly regular rows. "Ruby was originally well out from Diamond, and her weather must always have been severe. I would say that even here at the equator, the climate would have been equivalent to the upper-latitude ranges of Terra's or Aurora's north temperate regions. To thwart it, each window is fitted with a tight plug so efficiently made that they have remained in place during all the millennia since the dwellings were abandoned. The rooms I have been able to explore are to a one in perfect order. No drifted debris. No weather damage." She gave a little sigh. "Had any nonperishable artifacts been left behind, they would have survived with little or no hurt whatsoever."

The woman shrugged. It was pointless wasting time on regret. That those tragic people had left nothing after themselves must only be accepted.

"The ground floor appears to have been public space. There is an amphitheater chamber which looks as though it could have held the entire populace, plus two other much smaller rooms also obviously meant to accommodate gatherings. Besides these, there are numerous featureless spaces, perhaps intended for storage, and some which appear to have been stables to judge by the signs of the dividers once organizing them.

"Underground are five huge cisterns, empty now, of course, and twice that number of chambers which seem to have been granaries or vegetable bins. At least, I found traces of pollen in several of them, not a lot but too much to have come there accidentally."

"No grain or other produce, though?"

"Not so much as a seed." Her large eyes closed momentarily. "One of my colleagues once suggested in sport that the inhabitants had licked them clean. It was no longer funny once we realized it might actually have been true." She recalled herself. "Let us go inside, Taigue."

He nodded, chilled himself by the image the archopologist suggested, and drove the flier to the base of the building, traveling along it until they came to a metal door.

Banna slipped from her place and drew a big key from one of her belt pouches as she started running toward the barrier.

She hated the look of it. The door was jarring, a modern intrusion, but a strong defense was necessary against Ruby's winds and piercing cold. The original stone slab, once she had worked it loose after its ages of immobility, had moved well and was nothing if not efficient, but she had not dared risk damage to so ancient an artifact and so had at the culmination of her last expedition brought in expert craftsmen to remove and store it within and set this thing in its place.

It's lack of aesthetic appeal aside, the door worked well and easily, and she required only a few seconds to open it. Lis threw it wide and stood back, motioning for their vehicle to enter.

Chapter Thirteen

Murchu sat still after bringing the flier to a stop. It felt so inexpressibly good to be out of the wind, to be really free of it at long last, that for a moment he wanted nothing more than to remain where he was and allow the glory of that release to wash over him.

He roused himself after a couple of seconds. "Where would you like this stuff stowed, Doctor?"

"Right in here, at the back of the chamber, will do. This was probably a storeroom at one time, and it can serve in the same capacity again."

"What about him?" he asked, pointing toward the cam.

"He can go in one of the stables. There are no stalls, but, then, we have no other stock to worry him."

The man looked dubious. "I don't know, Banna. It's pretty cold in here, wind or no."

"Not for a cam. He will be well sheltered, free of direct drafts, and with a dry place on which to rest. Even food will be no real problem. He will have to share our rations, and unfortunately we cannot afford to be as generous with them as we were with that drink we let him have, but he will receive more than enough to keep him going and reasonably content."

The Ranger eyed her. "I'm still wondering about your lack of concern over our water supply. On a world as dry as Ruby of Diamond, an attitude like that is curious to say the least."

The Auroran reddened. "I am sorry, Taigue. I was showing off. You Rangers are usually so knowledgeable about every aspect of survival in the wild that I enjoyed being able to best you in this. It was foolish, I know—"

He only chuckled. "It does us no harm to be bested now and then, but what is the secret?"

"The ice. It is close to the surface all along the river bed, throughout much of this area, in fact. We have more than sufficient power to reach it and melt all we need. That was probably how the original inhabitants managed to procure water after the disaster, at least at first while they still had fuel, when they could locate no volcanic hot spot to release it for them."

Unloading the flier was no easier a task than packing it had been, but in the end, the pair had it emptied and their supplies stowed.

Because she knew the layout of the ruins, Banna Lis led the cam bull to the chamber where she intended to house him. She brought his evening's share of rations with her to help settle him, and by the time she was ready to leave him again, he was eating contentedly and looking quite as comfortable as she had predicted. The inflow from the single window she had opened to give him light and air would not trouble him where he was tied.

The archopologist sighed herself as she turned away. She had not banked on assuming such a charge, and although she had allowed a good margin for emergencies when she had laid in her supplies, she hoped she would be able to bring the animal back to the port and claim recompense for his feed soon. If not, she would be hard put to complete her work.

She shrugged. When she could do that was beyond her control. It was even beyond Murchu's, however eager he might be to finish up on Ruby and be away again. There was no point in worrying about it at this stage.

Before quitting the stable, the Auroran checked that the cam's chain was securely looped over the sturdy hook on which she had placed it.

She ran her fingers over the claw's remarkably smooth surface. She had remembered its presence in this room and so had chosen it as the place in which to house the beast, since it would allow them to keep him confined although, like the other chambers on this level, the stable had no door. It was a strange fixture cut from the otherwise smooth wall of the entrance for some obviously utilitarian reason. Had it served the very purpose to which she was putting it? The height seemed about right, given what she had surmised about Ruby's people. True, there was nothing like it in the other two stables she had discovered, but that might only mean a different sort of animal had been housed in those. She would have to see what evidence presented itself as she examined more of the rooms down on this level. It was a great pity she had discovered the site, the prize of Ruby's ruins, so late into her last expedition. There had been little time left to explore it then.

Her mind was still occupied with her work when she returned to the storeroom a few minutes later.

Taigue had used the time well. He had separated the items they would need to set up their camp and had bound them into four crude but secure packs. He nodded his greeting to the woman, then gave his attention back to the stairs, or ladder, he had been studying when she returned.

Carved into the wall itself, it consisted of a central pole about fifteen inches across. On either side of this were broad, flat steps. He shook his head. There was some inward slope to them, but it was quite apparent both hands and feet would be needed to ascend or descend it. Those ancient Rubians had been a hardy, lively group if this was how they moved around in here, he thought, as his mind pictured the almost countless journeys and burdens that were part of daily life in any community, however material-poor, and there was no evidence these folk had been that before tragedy had struck down their world.

"This is the only way up?" he asked, hoping the archopologist would be able to tell him of some easier mode of access. There was no reason to assume this was the main point of entrance to the upper levels merely because it was the first room they had encountered down here.

"No, but the others are all like it."

"That means two trips, then," he said, suppressing any display of the weariness he felt. She was just as tired. "We'll have to cart everything up on our backs."

"I know," Banna agreed ruefully. "That is why I camp on the second level rather than on the top floor, although the scenery would be better up there."

"Why not stay here altogether?"

"Because we really can make a warmer camp up there. Besides, I do like to have some view." She hesitated, not wanting to sound like a total inner-system vacuum brain. "There is a beauty in Ruby. I like to look out at her, try to make myself one with her. It seems somehow to help me understand a little better those who once lived here."

The Ranger-Captain did not look at her oddly, as if she had said something strange. He merely nodded slowly. "It's like that with us, too, when we are sent to study some planet, especially when we like her or find her particularly intriguing."

He took the small, powerful raditorch she handed him. It was fastened to a head strap, and he immediately slipped it into place as if it were a miner's helmet lamp. They would want the comfort of good light during the climb, particularly on the darkest stretch, when they were passing through the thick floor dividing the two levels.

"You know," he remarked suddenly, "It wouldn't surprise me if the Rubians weren't nocturnal or partly nocturnal. The gloom in here wouldn't be nearly as oppressive then even with a minimum of artificial illumination. Those members of the population active by day probably wouldn't have had to use any at all while they kept to windowed rooms."

Banna looked at him in surprise. "You could very well be right. It would make sense in a place like this. I am ashamed to say I never thought of it. —You are good at my business, Taigue Murchu."

"Why shouldn't I be?" he countered. "A Ranger likes to explore planets and learn what makes their inhabitants tick and think, humans as well as animals."

"All the same, I do not imagine most of your kind are as capable as you. I should enjoy working with you on an actual expedition, Captain, and you may put credits down I would not say the same thing to every individual I meet, outside my profession or within it."

"I'd like that as well," Taigue responded seriously. "We appear to be attracted to many of the same things, to the same aspects of a question. It would be interesting to try unraveling a few of them as a team."

He looked away. He was not likely to be given any such opportunity, conditions in the ultrasystem being what they were. His sense of regret was surprisingly sharp, and as much to distract himself as to cover the extent of his disappointment, he glanced back in the direction from which she had come. "You didn't leave that poor beast lying in total darkness, did you?"

"Of course not! There is a window, which I opened for him. This place is well designed, and he will take no chill from it."

Lis hoisted the makeshift pack nearest her onto her shoulders and pointed to a second one. "Up with you, Captain Murchu, or I shall begin to think you are afraid of heights."

"Hah!" He grabbed the bundle and made for the ladder.

"Careful," she cautioned. "Go easy. The steps are a little strange for our kind."

The Ranger had scarcely begun his ascent before he realized her warning was justified. The stairs were wide and straight, but they did not feel right, natural, to him. Their placement and the distance between the risers was odd, enough so to require his concentration until he had grown a little more accustomed to them. Those who had fashioned them had differed considerably in size and perhaps in basic build from Terra's offspring.

Despite that strangeness and the care it demanded, it was not long before he reached the second level. "Hand rails of some sort would've been a friendly gesture," he remarked as he reached down to assist the woman.

"Rubians were probably so agile and so accustomed to this place that they did not require them," the archopologist responded reasonably as they both scrambled to their feet. "I suppose it comes naturally when you do it every day of your life. Sure as space is black, they would have me bettered by a light year. –That opening to the right is the one we want."

Murchu passed through the entrance she indicated. It was not as well finished as those of the public spaces below, but there was no doubting its artificial origin or its purpose. How had it been closed, he wondered. Door, stone plug or slab, a fabric or beaded curtain? The indentations around the opening suggested any of those possibilities, or perhaps a combination of them.

The walls of the room in front of them were smooth and roughly circular. The chamber was about twelve feet in diameter and seven high. A bench-like structure approximately a foot tall and two deep circled the place save where the wall was broken by entrances to the common hall outside and to four other satellite chambers. The center of the floor was darker than the rest and dipped down in a distinct hollow where he imagined the hearth had once been located.

He turned to help his companion, who had followed him inside, but she smiled and waved him away. "Have a look around first. I want to see what we can accomplish with what we lugged up before we have to go for the next load."

The man needed no further invitation. He ducked into the first of the side chambers, one of those the Auroran had described as niches.

It proved to be unremarkable, absolutely plain and quite small, only four feet wide and seven deep with a roof no more than five feet from the floor at its highest point in the center.

The other rooms were identical to that one. By the time he had finished examining the last of them, Banna had set up and activated the stove in the old fire hole and was beginning to loosen the tent from its travel fastenings.

He hastened to help her with some embarrassment. "I'm sorry, Banna. I should've been attending to business and left the exploring until later."

The woman laughed at him. "Nonsense, friend. Have you not been telling me that exploring is your business? Besides, I told you to check the apartment out."

She pointed to the plugged window. "It can get very airless in these chambers, and I should like to save the charges in the raditorches. Could we chance opening that, at least by day?"

Murchu hesitated, then nodded. "Aye, by day."

The Ranger-Captain went over to the window. He studied the plug carefully and tried its fit before removing it. It slid out easily in his hands.

His expression was somber as he set it on the floor beside him. "Any light leakage at night could be the end of us," he warned. It would flag the chamber they were using, and it would be no great feat of marksmanship to send a blaster bolt set at broad beam through an opening this size. Their enemies could be counted upon to be able to shoot more than straight enough to accomplish that much.

"The tent is shielded, so there should be no problem unless we go wandering around ourselves." Her eyes flickered to the niche opposite her. "We could move into one of those if you prefer," she remarked doubtfully. "We would be cramped, but we should also be considerably warmer, and we would have almost no worries about escaping light."

"No!" Murchu swore at himself. He might as well have told her he would sooner sleep naked in one of the storage rooms below than tented in one of those dark boxes as long as the choice was his to make.

The woman did not notice his vehemence. She herself found the narrow rooms too claustrophobic, too like sepulchers, for her taste and had from the beginning preferred the chillier hospitality of the main chamber to their greater heat-retaining abilities. That her companion shared her lack of enthusiasm for them struck her as purely natural.

The off-worlders returned to the ground floor for the remaining two packs Taigue had assembled and then finished preparing their base, taking care to do the job well. This would be Banna's permanent camp while she remained on Ruby of Diamond.

Working together, they were not long in raising the tent. In that short time, even before they had finished arranging its interior for maximum comfort and convenience, the carefully designed Arctic stove had fulfilled its mission so well that they were able to strip off their jackets.

Murchu leaned back against one of the supporting poles and closed his eyes. "Space, that feels good. The cold had gone in right to my marrow."

"To mine as well. It was a nasty time, but we should be all right from here on." She yawned and stretched. "I suppose some dinner would be in order." Culinary duties had fallen to her that day.

The Ranger concealed his lack of interest, not wishing to make yet another display of weakness in front of her. It was not the archopologist's fault that he could summon no desire for the tasteless concentrates which were so frequently the mainstay of his existence. Banna Lis could not enjoy them very much, either. She probably cared even less for them than he did, accustomed as she was to some of the finest cuisine in the Federation. He had no right to grumble because she had nothing more palatable to offer.

"In an effort to break the silence which had fallen between them as Banna fished the makings of their evening meal out of the pack where he had stowed them, Tigue said, "I know your reports indicate there was nothing of the sort, but I was still rather hoping to stumble onto a painting or mosaic in one of those rooms. I was riding a comet's tail with that, I guess."

She smiled sympathetically. "It is a feeling I share, friend. I dream of making such a discovery every time I enter a room for the first time, something that would tell us how they lived, what they actually looked like, but I cannot believe I shall succeed. The visible arts do not seem to have developed at all on Ruby, not in a permanent form."

"Every intelligent species exhibits the desire to create," he argued.

"Granted, but it does not always reveal itself in the same manner. The Rubians may have expressed theirs exclusively in verbal form or in small, personal items or in body ornamentation. However," she concluded wistfully, "hope remains as long as there are parts of the ruins still to be explored."

"I, for one, wish you good hunting, Banna Lis. The mystery of these people is one I should very much like to see solved."

"It never will be, not in full."

Conversation lagged after that as each began to sort out his own belongings, organizing them for convenient use in their cramped quarters.

The warmth of the air and the smell of the heating food worked on the weary Patrol agent like a drug, but he shrugged off the comfortable lassitude gripping him and reached for his personal kit. He removed a jar of washing cream and a towel from it along with a spare set of clothes and went to the apartment's entrance. Tired as he was, he wanted to remove the grime and sweat of the journey before settling down. There should be time enough to put himself in order before their meal was ready if he did not delay.

Delaying was the last thing he was likely to do, he thought wryly as he stepped into the corridor outside. The artificial cave might make a bleak, Spartan residence, but it was relatively comfortable thanks to their stove. Its heat did not penetrate this far.

He grimaced. At least, the passage was reasonably draft free. That would work to his good when he stripped down.

Perhaps it did, but all the same, Taigue gasped as the frigid air hit his bare skin.

There was no need to be putting himself through all this, he thought irritably before sighing and continuing. He would not be freezing out here had he partnered with another Ranger, but Banna Lis was not that. She was not even a Regular. She was a civilian, more definitely a civilian than the citizens of any of those planets he normally defended. The capable, strong-willed comrade he was coming to know was balanced by the brilliant, influential inner-system scientist and author he had first met and with whom he had traveled during the initial stages of their journey to Ruby of Diamond. He could not forget that, and he had to treat with her in accordance with her status.

Besides, he thought suddenly, the archopologist would be wanting to wash and change into fresh things as well, and he knew she would not willingly do so in front of him. Aurorans were notoriously circumspect about making any display of themselves, even those who had enlisted in the Navy. It was better to take on the full lash of the cold again himself than to force her out into it.

He worked quickly, massaging the cream into his skin and toweling it off as it broke down into the bubbling semiliquid that lifted off sweat and dirt as if by magic. What he really wanted was an old-fashioned bath, preferably a very hot one, or a long session under Patrol-quality steam jets, but he might as well try to catch moonbeams as expect to find such luxury on this undeveloped world even under optimum conditions. As matters stood, he should consider himself flaming lucky to be given this opportunity at all.

The Ranger-Captain frowned at the mental reminder of the deadly serious work before him and of the difficulties he faced in accomplishing it. The contraband, chemicals and equipment, would not be stored too far from the port, of that, he instinctively felt certain, but the task of locating them seemed enormous, beyond any hope. Worse, even as he acknowledged this in his heart, a cold fear gripped him, a warning that time might be running short on him, far shorter than he had originally imagined.

How in the name of space was he to begin at all without the vaguest clue to start him off?

Murchu forcibly quelled the rush of despair threatening to sweep him. Surrender to that, and he would paralyze himself. He was trained to conduct a systematic search, whether it be for missing people or missing cargo. He would have to apply those techniques here and hope they bore fruit quickly, quickly enough.

He finished as rapidly as he could and hurried into his clothes. Despite the chilling he had taken, he felt refreshed, and he returned to the apartment entrance with a light step, as if he were beginning the day instead of nearing the end of a most trying one.

He paused outside, not wanting to burst in on the Auroran prematurely. "Banna, are you ready for company?"

"I am decent again. Come in before you freeze. Supper is ready."

Chapter Fourteen

Taigue sat beside the archopologist and accepted the plate she held out to him more eagerly than he would have thought possible earlier. He found he was hungry after all.

Despite his restored appetite, his attention was not really on the food, though he pretended it was fixed there. He could scarcely restrain himself from staring at his companion openly, like some planet-bound boy unaccustomed to the wonders the stars had wrought on humanity over the millennia.

Banna had indeed washed and changed as he had, but although she was fully dressed again, she had not bothered to refasten her hair. It now lay in a burnished copper flame on her back and left shoulder.

It was the first time he had seen it free like this. Always before, she had kept it under the firm discipline of a spacer's braid or in one of the exotic creations favored by the fashion of her homeworld. Custom and practicality both forbade her wearing it loose, but he had to admit its beauty was astonishing.

Banna Lis herself was beautiful. He had somehow not recognized that fact before now, though he had duly noted the striking perfection of her facial features and lithe body on their first encounter in her office on Aurora. Her strange, pallid complexion with its tracery of veins had effectively blinded him to the rest on all but a purely intellectual level.

He scowled. Beauty was relative in the Federation with its populations of basic Terrans, mutants of every degree, exoTerran humans, and nonhumans who were the equal of his kind but whose species had risen from other roots entirely. Each had its own standards, its own ideals, physical as well as cultural and intellectual. Malkites might be regarded by most others as overmuscled and altered almost to the point of caricature, but they were drawn to their own, and, in turn, they viewed prototypical Terrans as puny and bloodless, unattractive in the extreme. So it was with every race and subrace.

He cringed inwardly. If he had inadvertently insulted this woman despite all his service breeding and experience . . .

He stopped himself. No. He was not guilty of that. He had displayed no attraction to her, but it was no more than she would have expected from a man of prototypical human stock. They worked well together with no underlying hostility simmering in either of them, though by the Spirit of Space, Banna Lis was entitled to some resentment for the way he had forced his company on her. If she noticed his lack of physical interest, it was it was what she would have anticipated and which she probably welcomed. People who roamed the great void of space had learned very early in their exploration of the stars, so early it was now inviolable, instinctive law for all those traveling in space, that great discretion was required in their intergender behavior, even in their thoughtways, if intolerable, potentially deadly tensions were not to develop during their long voyages in extremely close quarters.

Banna, for her part, felt her companion's eyes on her and kept her own on her hands to avoid broadcasting her embarrassment. She could guess well enough what the Ranger thought of her, especially now, when she lacked even the garments and accents to emphasize at least her status.

For a moment, her anger rose. Murchu was no prize himself, either, not even by his own race's standards, but she could still like and admire him.

She gripped herself before her displeasure could become visible. Taigue had given every indication that he appreciated her for what she was. It was not his fault he did not also find her desirable. She stared at her battered nails in disgust. She would probably not even draw one of Aurora's sons at the moment.

As the Ranger continued to watch her, he realized the archopologist's own thoughts were on her appearance as well.

They were not nearly as favorable as his to judge by the way she unconsciously shook her head at the sight of her short unpainted nails, now much the worse for wear after their several bouts with her supplies and the work of dismantling and making camp.

Murchu was not so foolish as to tell her he found her more attractive as she was, but he wanted to say something. The thought that Banna should doubt herself in any sense infuriated him.

"You're quite amazing, you know," he declared suddenly. "Just about everyone's bilingual at the least, but you're the first person I've met who is truly bi-lived."

"What in space or beyond it do you mean by that?"

"You're an Auroran to the hilt, yet you are also unquestionably a woman of the rim."

"Surely you have to play your share of roles."

"Aye, but they're just that for the most part, roles, and usually they're variations on a basic theme. I'm a Patrol-bred Ranger of Terran extraction serving on the rim where I belong. You're something more, equally the celebrity holding court on that transgalactic and the scientist well able to live and work alone on some of the most unforgiving planets in the ultrasystem. I confess now that the first does not awe me, but this part of you impresses all the Federation's hells out of me."

"I do not know if I should be pleased," Lis teased, her eyes sparkling. "Do you also envision me behind an automated plough, or perhaps a traditional one?"

The man wanted to respond that she would look equally good with either, but he only smiled. "You're no agrarian or miner, Banna Lis, but in your own capacity, you do belong out here. I only wish the same could be said of a great many of the Regulars who get transferred to the edge of the ultrasystem, and for some of those civilians trying to settle newly opened worlds, too, despite rigorous precolonization testing, though most of the latter do pull up stakes in pretty short order when they discover their mistake." He grimaced. "They usually have a hard time of it and often give everyone else a hard time before they do."

"Then I do thank you for the compliment, Captain," the Auroran said gravely. "I had not considered myself in that light. I am glad you do."

He was quiet for a short while. "Do you always work alone?"

"Frequently. Even a small expedition can be prohibitively expensive, and as you know, getting hands can range from difficult to virtually impossible depending upon the location involved. Help is necessary when any more than two or three scientists want to work a site, particularly if their disciplines are different."

"There is no second one?" he persisted. "No companion of choice?"

She frowned slightly, realizing what he was asking. "Not now. —I have been a widow for these last four years. You must be aware of that."

The Ranger shook his head. "No. I was told nothing about you beyond what I had to know. You were investigated, of course. The magnitude of this case made it essential we ascertain you weren't involved in the theft, but I wasn't given the results save that you were clear of suspicion. I had no right to know anything more. A citizen's business is entirely his or her own unless it's likely to have bearing on an assignment."

"Hearing that makes me feel a bit better about you people," she admitted.

"Your husband? What happened to him? The War? That is, if you don't mind discussing it," he added hastily. A great many people disliked probing their wounds. He wanted to learn more about this woman, not to interrogate her.

"I do not mind. –Greg Maneli was an archopologist as well. In fact, we won our doctorates from the University of Aurora at the same time. He was hit with Quandon Fever while we were at an isolated dig. It was a mutation that gravely challenged our shots. Mine held it off. His did not. Greg had always tested sensitive to the virus anyway, and this variety was extraordinarily virulent and fast acting." Her voice dropped. "He went from well to dead in less than three days. There was nothing I could do for him myself and no way to bring help to him rapidly enough to save him." Her brows creased. "The Patrol tried, but they reached us a week too late."

"That was a rough charter," Taigue said softly. This was a grief he could well understand. Too well. Loss of those they loved was a misfortune everyone shared in these dark, violent days. In Lis' case, the despair of having to watch helplessly while death took its victim had added to her pain.

Banna accepted the sympathy he was offering. "Time does heal, praise the One ruling all of us. We could not survive at all if it did not, I suppose."

The searing anguish of those first months had faded, she thought, and she could look back at the tragedy now without grief tearing the heart out of her, but the small things remained. The memory of a word or gesture or habit could still jump out at an unexpected moment to wring her heart with longing.

The Auroran willed the thought to pass. "I am not alone in the universe, of course. I do have near kin."

"Parents? Siblings?"

"Yes. I am close with my parents, both of whom are respected surgeons. I live with them when I am on Aurora. As for siblings, my sister Anna died trying to push the Arcturians out of Marion Sector, but I do have a brother. Jacques is Doctor of Comparative Sociology at the University of Aurora."

She smiled at his grimace. "He is really not so bad, although we do have our differences now and then."

"I'll put a few credits down that you do," the man muttered sourly. "He's a confirmed planet hugger, I expect?"

"Oh, strictly." Banna laughed. "Sometimes I believe he thinks my profession is not quite respectable because it requires me to go off-world so frequently." The archopologist eyed him curiously. "You Stellar Patrol people do not care for those in his field, do you?"

"Some of their fine pronouncements make practical law enforcement rather difficult when they get taken too seriously by government brass. The Tatarina disaster did us that much good at least. A pirate is universally regarded as a pirate, and we have more or less a free hand in dealing with them."

"Thanks to the news nanos of the massacre," she said shrewdly. "It was no accident they were so graphic, was it?"

"No. Reporters were permitted in to cover the story only on condition that they would record everything as they found it and that there would be absolutely no editing of the material out of consideration for their viewers' sensibilities. It was well past time for the inner systems to be shocked back into awareness of what life is like elsewhere in the Federation and what it might too easily become for them if they remained complaisant much longer."

His tone had grown harsh as he spoke, and Banna gave him a measuring look. "I did not realize there was such bitterness against us," she said quietly. "Or is this just you?"

"No. I'm talking general feeling, but I didn't mean to detonate like that." Murchu leaned forward a little. "The fault lies with those planets' very success. It's been centuries since they were first settled, and now they have the entire power of the ultrasystem to guard them. Too much safety, too great security over too long a span of time, can be more a curse to a people than a blessing. Our sort soften without physical challenge, soften in every sense. Gradually the purpose which drove their ancestors and formed and guided their societies faded, replaced by newer fashions which could never have come into existence in the face of danger and difficulty. Theory, however admirable in original intent, began to replace reason. —It's a sad alteration to see happen to a once-strong race, Banna, and it puts a real burden on the rest of us."

"That is a little unfair."

"Is it? Setting aside some of the half-finned laws your 'civilized' planets have shoved through the Senate to plague us, look at what happened at the outset of the War. It was the rim member worlds and colonies who responded to the call to arms almost exclusively until the steady stream of Arcturian victories finally shook the inner planets out of their happy oblivion and drove home the fact that we would all be groveling in some war prince's shadow if they didn't do something to help the Federation—and do it right fast."

Her head lowered. That charge was accurate. It was a shameful blot on Aurora's history and on the history of most of her near neighbors, one which could not be denied or refuted.

The officer relented. The archopologist was not responsible for what the previous generation had done or failed to do, and her family had certainly carried its part through her sister, paying the full price for their involvement.

"The citation lists prove most of those planets made up for their slow start, but some resentment does remain. It's bound to still be felt, particularly among those peoples whose troops bore the brunt of the early assaults and suffered the heaviest losses while so many of those they defended did not so much as pause in their feasting and playing to offer a brief prayer for their sake."

His hand reached out to brush hers. "None of that reflects on you or yours." He smiled. "Not even on your illustrious brother."

She smiled in her own turn but said gravely, "Surprisingly enough, in his own way, he would be glad to hear you say that."

"However blameless, he's of little use to you in the field. Isn't there anyone you'd like to take on as a permanent . . . associate?"

The archopologist shook her head. "No. I have not looked for a companion like that since I lost Greg. My profession, with all the travel and hardship it entails, is not an attractive one to most of those outside it, and the few people I know in the field whom I might have considered in that light have already formed such attachments."

Her dark eyes fixed on him. "Now, Captain Murchu, I have responded to your questions. I expect a return in kind."

"That's fair enough. Fire away."

"I have dealt with Rangers before, but they worked in pairs or in larger teams. I thought that was standard procedure. What about you?"

"It's not inviolable procedure, though we usually prefer to have at least one comrade's help on a mission. My official partner died, oh, thirteen months ago. Natural causes. A massive coronary." His mouth hardened momentarily. "It struck him down three hours after receiving a complete all-clear on his annual physical."

"Taigue, I am sorry!" she exclaimed. "I know what a shock that must have been."

"It did bring home the fact of my own mortality." He did not say what the loss of the man who had saved his life and whose life he had saved on occasions nearly too numerous to count had meant to him. He did not have to say it. Banna Lis knew already.

"You have not chosen or been assigned anyone else to work with you?"

He shook his head. "Not yet. I've had only a couple of short missions since then, and I wound up in the hospital after the last. I was just starting to look for someone suitable when I was sent out on this business."

"Family?" she asked. "Do you have anyone?"

"Aye. I'm not as fortunate as you in that my parents are dead. They blew themselves up ramming a pirate cruiser over Zora." He saw her look of horror. "They were Patrol agents, Banna. It was that or see the mines blasted, and it was the way they would've wanted to go had they designed the course of their lives—quick, to good purpose, and together. Theirs was a love match for the whole voyage, and neither would've cared to survive the other by very long." His head lowered but raised again in the next instant. "As you said, time heals. They died a lot of years ago, and memories of them are good now and welcome."

"Your other kin?"

"A brother with the Exploratory Force and a cousin with the Regulars. My sister's a turncoat. She went into the Navy." He grinned, unable to mask his pride. "She's just made Commando-Captain."

"You Murchus are quite a clan, apparently." The Auroran was impressed and did not try to conceal the fact.

Another question had been stirring in her mind almost from the beginning of their association. Normally, she would have had to leave it unasked, but since he had broached the same topic himself, she had the right to raise it as well. "You are not married or otherwise allied?"

"No. I had planned to face the altar after I graduated from basic training, but my fiancée broke it off. She was a civilian, and she had the maturity, girl though she still was, to realize it would never work. She couldn't stand my schedule or long absences or the fear I might never return from my current or next mission. I was furious at the time, but since then, I've had to admit she was the one to show sense. She saved us both from inevitable disaster."

"You were young yourself then. In all the time since—"

He shrugged. "Civilians find joining with someone in my line of work an even less attractive prospect than involving themselves with someone in yours." Stellar Patrol Command recognized the personal as well the physical difficulties encountered by their agents and generally teamed unpaired young male and female cadets when they were sworn in as yeomen, knowing nature could probably be depended upon to take its course in the months of close association and rough, perilous service ahead. That had not been done with him, then or later, perhaps because his engagement had been broken too near graduation to arrange such a partnership. Apart from a couple of very peripheral, short-lived alliances, he had never tried to introduce a relationship of that intimacy into a life he found complex enough as it stood. "As for seeking someone within the Patrol, I simply never really bothered to look. There was always too much else to do."

"That is a pity, Taigue Murchu. You have deprived yourself of a great deal."

Himself and another. The Ranger-Captain was a good man and basically a nice one. He deserved to know the warmth and fulfillment of a union like the one she had once shared with Greg, and he would strive to secure and maintain its bond once he had committed himself to it. She would think very little of the woman who would not work with him at that task, only assuming he chose someone able to accept the unquestioned challenge posed by his profession.

It would accomplish nothing to belabor the point apart from embarrassing them both. She set her empty plate aside and glanced at the timer on her wrist. "It is late now, and I want to start work as soon as possible tomorrow."

He nodded. "I was about to suggest knocking out myself."

"We should stand watch again tonight?"

"Aye, though it's not likely we'll have any visitors unless the lads back at the spaceport have come to suspect us since we left them. As matters stand, their wisest course is simply to ignore us and let us forget about them."

"I shall take the first turn. I am tired enough that I will not want to rouse again once I am asleep, and I do not want to put your sympathy to the test by having to wake me."

The Ranger smiled. "I doubt I'd fail. I'm too spent myself. But have it your way by all means." His eyes fixed on their small, powerful interstellar transceiver, which occupied the tent wall opposite the place where they were sitting. "You will report in first?"

"Of course. As soon as we stow our mess kits."

"Don't forget the code sequence I told you to use."

"Have no fear, Captain, your message will be faithfully transmitted."

Taigue's reminder of the true purpose behind his presence on Ruby roused Banna out of her blissful inactivity. She grunted as she turned a little too sharply. "I pity myself tomorrow. My muscles are already saying some unpleasant things about the abuse I've heaped on them lately."

"They're in good company."

"You are a Ranger!" she exclaimed, taken aback by the idea that such commonplace labor should trouble him.

"A Ranger who doesn't spend every spare moment in training," he told her. "I'll probably come off a bit better than you, but rest assured I'll have reason to remember our activities of today." He reluctantly shifted out of his comfortable position. "Let's hurry and finish up here. That sleeping bag is beginning to look very desirable."

Chapter Fifteen

Banna awoke to find the tent empty the following morning. She dressed quickly and rerolled her sleeping bag, then left their quarters to search for her companion.

Taigue Murchu was standing by the window. He was leaning against the wall and gazing pensively out on the dry red world below.

There was nothing in his manner or expression to suggest alarm, but she approached him carefully all the same, watching that she did not startle him or expose herself to the view of anyone who might have distance lenses trained on the small opening.

"See anything?" she whispered.

"No. All is quiet, as I expected. I was only thinking about those who abandoned this place, wondering what actually happened to them."

The archopologist and her colleagues back on Aurora had supplied some of the details and had made a number of reasonable inferences based on the information she had uncovered during her first expedition.

To judge by the lack of structural damage, the inhabitants of the complex had probably survived the initial cataclysm with little or no injury, but cold and the lack of free-flowing water must have forced them to leave it very shortly thereafter.

The rest was conjecture, albeit supported by the testimony of the other ruins thus far discovered. Both were of a much later date and were smaller and of more hasty, less refined construction that stressed the conservation of heat.

According to the archopologists' theory, the populace had split into several bodies, most likely already existing political, religious, or kinship groups, that had struck out independently in search of thermal or volcanic hot spots, which had become Ruby's most valuable resource.

Some groups, at least, had found suitable sites, places where the planet's inner fires supplied the heat to combat the bitter cold and to melt the ice that was the repository of her once-plentiful water. There they had settled, supporting themselves, though at a much more primitive level, by agriculture and probably by whatever stock they had managed to save as well. Those using the two sites Banna had studied had survived for several generations, but their hold on life was precarious, and disaster had eventually come upon both.

Increased volcanism in the vicinity was deemed to have doomed the first. Although the dwellings had weathered the challenge, the fields and perhaps a good part of the population apparently had not. In any event, no further work had been done at the site after the critical eruption.

The evidence was not so clear with respect to the second, but the archopologist believed the heat source sustaining it had simply failed, leaving the populace at the mercy of cold and thirst. With available sources of fuel probably nearly exhausted by that time, the people would no longer have had the ability to extract sufficient water to sustain their community.

What had happened to them? What had happened to the other refugees from the mother ruin, those about whom they had as yet found no record? There was no such question about populations who had lived in Ruby's higher latitudes. They must have perished almost immediately from the insuperable cold, but these ones had been forced to fight on. How had they come to their end at last?

"How did they die?" Murchu asked aloud as he felt the woman draw up beside him. "Did they drag themselves on in the futile hope of finding a new heat source, falling one by one until the final strength of the last survivor gave out? Did they remain where they were or stop their hopeless search at some point, burn every dead stump they could find, every possession, and then expire in slow agony once their supplies were spent? Did they accept the inevitability of death and choose to pass out of life with dignity on their own terms, perhaps with the head of each household taking care of his dependents and then himself?"

She looked at him in amazement. "You really do care?"

"Aye," the Ranger replied stiffly. "My people, the Terran subrace whose blood I carry, are survivors. Even in prespace-colonization times, we had to face one trial after another, and that has been the mark of our history since. We're one of the major colonizing races, you see, the major one in point of fact. Our genes are significantly represented in the populations of at least three-quarters of Terran-seeded Federation planets. Just about anything that could happen to threaten a people has struck at one group or another of us. Most made it. Some did not. –You can put credits down that I empathize with those Rubians. We'd have died, too, had the same disaster hit us before we had the technology and the off-world contacts to meet it."

"Then you do understand what drives me so hard?" she asked softly. "Why I cannot bear that all knowledge of this talented, ill-starred people should be lost?"

"I do, Banna Lis. I understand." He looked at her somberly. "I know you can't answer my questions, not yet. Just make sure you get those answers, or try to get them, before you people finish with Ruby of Diamond."

"Archopologists do not abandon a puzzle because the bulk of the pieces are gone, my friend," she answered proudly. "We keep right on working, and occasionally the partial skeleton we have gets fleshed out, sometimes generations after the search began."

She glanced out the window, then turned decisively back to the tent. "That is for later, after we have settled your business."

"You've done your part already."

The Auroran eyed him coolly. "If the fate of an unknown people who vanished millennia ago can move me, Taigue Murchu, do you imagine I can remain oblivious to the needs of those in my own era? If anything, I am probably more conscious of what could be involved in this case than you or your superiors are. You speak of the Tatarina disaster, but I think you do not appreciate the full scope of it, not merely that a lot of people died there but that the race they were building died with them. The planet has been repopulated and will flourish again, but the original gene pool cannot be recovered. The losses were too great, and too much new blood had to be brought in.

"No natural accident caused that horror, and another of equal if different violence threatens again. The poisoned raklik will gut the strength of some unsuspecting planet or planets. The addiction of so many others among their citizens who survive the first wave of the disaster will complete the destruction of their civilizations. I did not ask or desire to be involved in a situation like this, but since it is the Creator's will that I am, I intend to do whatever lies in my power to resolve it. I could not face myself if I did otherwise."

"Put it on freeze, Doctor. I don't intend to drag you into battle with me, but you'll do your share. At the very least, I'll be wanting to mine your brain more deeply than I already have." He sighed and shook his head. "For a while there, I'd nearly forgotten what brought me to Ruby of Diamond."

Banna Lis smiled. "I doubt that, Captain. You may prefer some aspects of your job to others, but you are a Stellar Patrol agent born and bred. I cannot even imagine your forgetting a mission as critical as this one." She paused. "You have not forgotten it, either. If anything, you are more concerned now than you were at its outset."

His brows raised, but then he nodded. "Aye. Aye, I am. It's a feeling, a gnawing, rodent fear, that time is racing by us, racing by us fast. It keeps growing stronger—"

He drew a sharp, hissing breath. "Of course! Banna, curse me for a fused-circuited microwit. A probie cadet wouldn't have missed this."

"What is it?" she demanded in alarm.

"I thought the space scum back in the port were on-world guarding the contraband. What if they've come for it instead and are merely waiting for orders or to be sure of us before grabbing and lifting with it?"

"Those needle noses are small for that if there is as much material involved as you have given me to understand," the Auroran answered after several moments' horrified thought.

"They stole it in the first place," he reminded her.

"They did, but there would have been no room left on either of them for anything else, not even additional armaments or fuel. You've admitted one prime reason your intelligence people targeted Ruby as a possible interim site for storing the contraband is because she's relatively close to Gamma. The renegades wouldn't stash it someplace with a Patrol base only a planetfall away otherwise."

Her expression darkened. "They'll have to lift with everything at once when they make their move. Running a shuttle service, returning several times to empty out the stockpile, would be too dangerous with government activity increasing on both Sapphire and Emerald. They also have to have another drop site reasonably near to hand," Banna concluded shrewdly.

"Rest assured they do, probably where they'll turn everything over to the masterminds who hired them. Those raiders we encountered did not plan the robbery, though they doubtless participated in the execution of it. We can also be certain they're not betraying their employers and planning to abscond with the take themselves. Without access to the facilities necessary to process and then market the stuff, their cargo would be nearly worthless to them. My guess is they'll either transfer everything to a larger vessel in space or deliver it to its buyer at some port fairly near at hand."

"Maybe the buyer will come for it here," she suggested.

He shook his head. "No. He or they won't risk that. Those sons will want as little contact as possible with their hirelings and none at all anywhere with a Navy or Stellar Patrol base near at hand."

"Will they, the bosses, terminate the raiders then?" she asked thoughtfully. "That would remove the danger of exposure and reduce the expense of the operation."

Taigue's brows raised. "You do have a conniving mind, Doctor Lis. –No. Death during the course of a raid is commonplace. Betrayal is another matter. Word of that would spread through the less savory segments of the ultrasystem faster than quick plague through an unvaccinated population. Even only a strong suspicion would result in the culprits finding themselves without support or marketing operations and probably with a few assassins on their tails as well."

"You are sure about all this?" the Auroran asked him. "I mean about them being ready to lift with everything."

"No. I don't know enough to be certain. There's no evidence to support my belief, but it feels right. It feels all too right."

He straightened. "I'll have to commandeer your services for the morning, I fear."

"That goes without saying," she snapped impatiently. Banna hesitated. "What are you going to do, Taigue? There are ten pirates between those two ships, nine since you have already eliminated one of them, and only the pair of us—"

"Neither of whom is a Commando?"

"Commando?" she replied bitterly. "I am not even a competent comrade. What use am I against those thugs? All the wishing in the universe cannot supply me with battle skills and the training to use them effectively."

The Ranger-Captain privately believed Lis would make a considerably better showing than she imagined, but he did not contradict her. The last thing he wanted was to put this woman into a position of proving or disproving that statement.

"I'm not looking for a fight myself. It's the contraband, primarily the chemicals, I'm after on this round, not the raiders. At this stage, I think my plan must be to destroy rather than try to recover them."

"Will you be able to do that?"

"Hopefully. There isn't that much choice. I know enough to blow the lot if I can only find out where it's all being stored. Fortune willing, I won't have to start and end a war in the process."

"You don't think you'll have to fight?" she demanded incredulously.

"It's possible I won't. Everything depends on how soon the raiders intend to move. If we can reach the cargo before they return to claim it, we should be away with it."

"What about sentries?"

"There shouldn't be any. Why post active guards on a planet without a population to interfere with them?"

"I had not considered that." The Auroran frowned. "How are we to locate the stockpile? I have been puzzling about that since you first told me about this business. Ruby is a big place, and I do not even know how to begin breaking down the field for you."

The man shrugged. He had come to some terms with his own earlier fears and now strove to put hers to rest. "It won't be easy, and you can lay credits down that I've been doing a lot of thinking on the subject, but the job isn't as bad as it seems at first glance. For one thing, we do not have to search the whole bloody planet. The fact that they had been using the cams proves the shipment's stashed somewhere on the equator and reasonably near the port."

"Why bother with them at all?" she asked curiously. "They have a flier."

"The same reason the Settlement Board is testing them. To save on fuel. A five-man fighter isn't blessed with unlimited hold space, and Ruby has no vast stores to offer. The animals are a viable alternative, but only within a certain area, or lost time would negate any other savings."

"That makes sense."

"We also know our target's on this side of the port."

"How— Oh, the cam again!" Naturally. The thieves had to have been traveling either to or from their hoard when they abandoned the beast. "Knowing that should help us."

"Immensely."

"There is still plenty of ground left," Banna reminded him.

"We can pare it down a bit farther. They wouldn't just drop the stuff out on an open plain, not if they had any better choice. A cave or good, broad ledge would be the preferred site, but they'd want at least broken, rock-strewn country where their cargo would blend in sufficiently to go unnoticed by airborne traffic passing nearby. They knew when they chose her that they'd be using Ruby for a relatively long period of time and that she does occasionally get a few legitimate visitors such as yourself and people from the Settlement Board."

"Even so—"

"Even so, we have a lot of ground to cover and little time in which to do it. That's where you come in. The site won't be so close to this place that we'd be likely to stumble on it accidentally, or they'd have stopped us from coming out in the first place, but you've got to have a pretty good idea of the territory around here, enough to fill in the charts I was given. They're flaming crude to put it mildly."

"I can do that much readily enough."

"It's all I require. The rest is up to me."

Suddenly, he slammed his hand against the wall. "Who am I trying to fool? You're as deeply involved as I am. Those space scum know where we are. If this sours at all, the consequences are going to fall as heavily on you as on me."

"That became an inevitable possibility once we found the raiders already on-world, did it not?" she asked quietly.

The gray eyes closed. "I never planned this. My superiors never planned it this way. I swear to you, Banna, you were to provide me with a cover and supply me with the kind of information I've just requested. That was to be the extent of your involvement in all this."

"Fate seems to have willed otherwise. You cannot be blamed for its decisions, especially since you are in exactly the same position your-self."

"That is part of my job."

"In a sense, it is part of mine as well," the archopologist reasoned slowly. "I am a citizen of the Federation and an adult human being. I have a responsibility to the people of this ultrasystem, and I am bound to fulfill it in whatever manner I can." Banna eyed him. "I think I told you nearly the same thing a few minutes ago," she observed.

She stopped herself, and when she spoke again a moment later, there was no anger or irritation in either her tone or her expression. She only smiled and shook her head when he started to apologize.

The tips of her fingers touched his where they still rested against the wall. "You are carrying a double load of that responsibility I mentioned. You are toting everything I do and that much more again thanks to your Stellar Patrol code. I do not envy you, my friend."

The woman withdrew her hand again quickly. "What do we do first?" she asked.

"Have breakfast," Taigue Murchu told her. "I think better on a full stomach."

Banna laughed. That was not the answer she had been anticipating, but it was so totally practical she knew she should have expected it. "I shall not be long rustling it up," she assured him.

"The turn is mine—"

"Perhaps the next meal," she told him. "Lay out what we need and then collect our gear for our day's work."

The Auroran's nose wrinkled as she went to their store of supplies. "I brought as much variety as I could, but rations are rations. I fear we shall be well tired of our menu long before the expedition ends."

Before even his own mission ended, the Ranger thought.

That was unavoidable. He could do no more than resign himself to it, and it behooved him to do so with reasonably good grace. He was not suffering alone in any of this.

Taigue shrugged. "No one working in this climate is likely to reject fuel because it would not adorn the tables of Hedon."

He flexed his shoulders, testing his muscles to see how much of the stiffness born of the previous day's labors still remained to plague him. There were a few twinges, but on the whole, he was pleased. He might be no cadet, but his body retained its resilience.

"We should be getting moving once we eat," he remarked. "We still have to see to our four-footed charge before we can set off on our own work."

Chapter Sixteen

Banna led the way to the chamber where she had stabled the bull, her expression growing darker with every step as they moved along the passageways of the long-dead civilization. The very shadows seemed to call to her, enticing and scorning because she could not give her attention to the mysteries shimmering in their depths.

Anger tightened her nerves, speeded the throb of her pulse. There was so much that needed to be done and so little time before dwindling supplies would force her to terminate her expedition. It would have been impossible to accomplish everything even under normal circumstances. Why in space had this problem been dropped on her, when all she wanted was to get on with her work and respond as she should to the lure of the unexplored chambers all around her?

The woman willed herself to quell her resentment. The threat of death and a slavery worse than any death hung over a multitude of people. What significance did her projects have in the face of that? Had she descended to such a level of selfishness that she would set publication or even her own intellectual satisfaction above human life and welfare?

She was glad she was moving several paces ahead of her companion with her face completely hidden from him. Whatever the other failings he might have, when it came to his responsibilities, Taigue Murchu's priorities were dead on course.

Her sister's priorities had been equally straight, and she had died for them . . .

Banna shivered. She did not want death to be her portion, not with so much of life still before her, and that might all too readily prove the end of this business. The very thought of facing down those space renegades filled her with sick horror.

Taigue saw the woman shudder but believed the cold to be the cause of it. There was no escaping it. Only inside their small tent were they truly warm. Everywhere else, Ruby's deadening chill remained a constant. The stout walls of the ancient structure freed them from the brutal lash of the wind, making it possible to live and work, but never in any degree of real comfort. Even with a stove close beside her, laboring for hours on end in essentially one cramped position could be no joy, and he marveled at the archopologist's tenacity in going on with her slow searching day after day for weeks at a stretch, all for the most intangible of goals, to increase humanity's store of knowledge about another, long-vanished race. He wondered if he would have the same solar steel in his spine were their positions reversed.

Solar steel? Banna Lis was pure titanone.

He pulled his thoughts back to the present as his companion's pace slowed.

"In there," she said, pointing. "He is right by the entrance."

The cam was lying down when they entered his stable, a dark, shaggy mound rising out of the smooth red stone of the floor, apparently oblivious to the chill. He had seemed to be asleep but roused almost as they stepped inside, and he shambled to his feet. His head stretched out toward them, his nostrils spread wide.

"He seems to have weathered the night in good form," Murchu conceded. "He's hungry now. Can you take care of feeding and watering him while I have a look at that leg?"

Banna glanced sharply at him, then at the animal. "Is something the matter with it?" she demanded with real concern.

The Ranger regarded her in surprise. Like the rest of their species, Aurorans took animals, home-grown and exotic, into their homes and hearts as pets, but even forgetting his size, there was nothing appealing about the cam. Taigue's nose wrinkled. Most assuredly not his smell.

The archopologist seemed to read his thoughts. "Oh by the towers of Siren," she said irritably, "I am not thinking of parading him along Aurora's boulevards at the end of a leash. I just do not want to see him abused or neglected while he is in my care."

"He should be fine. I only want to confirm no infection has set in and all the pieces are out of the wound. That was one fast bit of surgery I did on him yesterday."

She nodded. "I know. Sorry, Taigue. —Wait until he starts eating, or you might have trouble with him. He seems more energetic this morning after his supper and a night's rest."

The cam was that, the man thought as he poured the contents of the canteen he had carried with him into the basin Banna had provided the previous day for the purpose and left it for her to present to their patient. If anything was amiss with the injured leg, it was mechanical. There was no infection operating in the animal's system.

The bull settled down once the Auroran crumbled the rations she had brought for him and set them down in front of him. Taigue watched him a moment longer, pausing briefly to admire the finely worked hook to which he was fastened, then went behind him and carefully compared his legs. Both were set squarely on the floor, the bandaged one supporting the same weight as its undamaged mate. There was no sign of swelling or tenderness.

He set his first aid kit beside him. It probably would not even be necessary to replace the dressing, but he might as well be prepared. He hoped it would not be required. There was no use in annoying the big animal with unnecessary or repeated procedures. He had a feeling the cam would be none too pleased with any further interference with the hoof as it was.

Murchu took hold of the leg and sighed. It remained solidly in place, seemingly as firm as a tree anchored by a deep tap root. He would receive no cooperation from his patient this morning.

Spreading his legs to brace himself, he began to exert a strong upward pull on the limb.

It moved a little, but the cam grunted and shifted his full weight onto the bandaged limb. Even as he did, he let fly with the other leg, catching the man sharp and hard between the thighs.

Murchu went down with a muffled groan. He rolled out of range of a second strike but could do no more for the next several seconds than lie where he was and let the agony of the blow sear through him.

"Taigue!" The Auroran's voice was sharp with fear as she ran to him. "Space, what a knock! Are you all right?"

She slipped her arm under him and after a few moments managed to raise him to a sitting position. He leaned on her, his breath coming in sharp gasps while he fought to master the shock and pain.

At last, he took his weight back on himself. "I'll survive, I think."

Her dark eyes studied him anxiously. His face was still a sickly gray-green, and she thought it would be a while yet before he would be ready to try getting to his feet.

"Just stay put. I will be back in a few minutes." With that, she sprang up and darted from the stable.

True to her promise, the woman returned quickly, a flask in her hand. "Here. Get this into you. If ever a man looked like he needed a good, stiff drink, you do."

Taigue's hands were steady as he took it from her. "What is it?"

"Opaline. Auroran quality. Nothing like the half-poison you probably had to swallow back at the port. I keep it on hand for emergencies." She grimaced. "I think this qualifies."

The Ranger opened the flask and took a long pull of the fiery liquor. It was hot to the taste but well processed as she had promised and smooth to swallow. Within moments, he could feel it beginning to take the edge off the shock still gripping him. "Thanks, Banna. That's a galaxy better."

"I am glad I had it. —That was a nasty one."

"An accurate assessment, Doctor."

Banna smiled a little tightly. He was coming to himself again, though he would probably be hurting for some time to come. "I saw a cam do the same thing once before," she told him. "If it is any comfort to you, its handler told me such accidents occur with some frequency but they rarely affect a man's after-hours performance."

As she had intended, he responded with a quick if rather wan grin. "I might take that as a promise."

"Do not," she advised dryly. "I might suggest it to comfort a dying man, but you are very obviously going to live."

He took another drink, then recapped the flask and handed it back to her. "Thanks again, Doctor Lis. You scientific types come better equipped than I'd imagined."

"We do try." She got to her feet. "What now?"

"Finish examining that thankless—"

The Ranger-Captain looked sharply at the cam bull, his eyes narrowing. "Hold up a minute, Banna."

She sat beside him again. "What is wrong?"

"Nothing. I just remembered something you said yesterday. You were angry because our opponents didn't give this fellow a chance to follow after them at his own pace. Could he really do that? Find the stockpile by himself?"

The Auroran straightened. "Lead us to it?"

He nodded. "It could be our answer. Is it possible?"

Banna's lips tightened, and her head lowered. If only she knew more . . .

"I do not think so, Taigue," she said at last. "Cams can follow a familiar path, and I think they can scent one of their own kind for some distance, but how would he know where to go from here?"

Murchu was quiet for a few seconds. "I'd have to bring him back to the place where we found him and give him his head from there."

"He might just return to the spaceport."

"Aye. It would be a fifty-fifty chance, but if I keep him faced away from it, he could well go right. It's worth a trial anyway."

"Taigue?"

There was something in her tone which caused him to swing his attention fully to her. "What's the matter?"

"If your theory is correct, that shipment has been on-world for months. There would be no reason for the pirates to go near it with cams, or a flier, either, unless they were getting ready to move it all like you were thinking. In that case, they . . . they must have had the cargo, or a good part of it, on hand in the port when we arrived."

Taigue Murchu turned white, recognizing the logic of what the archopologist said. "I've been a blind man," he whispered. "I believed the second warehouse was also empty when it may well have been otherwise. That would explain the Albionan's panic. I've been thinking we had a little time, and instead we could have none. —By the Spirit ruling Space, the whole lot could be lost to us while I sit here."

"Probably not," the woman reasoned hastily, trying to quell her own growing dread. "The raiders should delay shifting everything off-world a while longer just to be certain no one followed us for any reason. They cannot afford to draw attention themselves at so crucial a point, can they, by getting into a fight or even by permitting anyone to see them lifting and maybe get a fix on their course? Perhaps we do have a few more days?"

There was fear in that last question, but if Banna's certainty had wavered, she had restored his balance. He nearly swept her into his arms before he caught himself. A woman of her grace would never permit such a liberty, but still, nothing could quell Tigue's broad smile. "You're thinking more like a Patrol agent than I am, Banna Lis! —Aye, we have time yet, or we do if I start earning my pay."

"What are you planning to do?"

Banna could feel her heart begin to pound as life and hope both surged back into her. The return of purpose in her companion was wonderful to witness, and with it came the conviction that there was a real chance in what had seemed like grasping at moonbeams a moment before. The Ranger-Captain was no shooting star, and if he still planned to go after their enemies, it was because he believed they could accomplish their purpose against them.

Taigue was already on his feet. He glared in the direction of the cam. "First, I'm going to finish checking out the cam, even though he's technically assaulted a Federation officer. After that, I'll put a call on secure beam to the Regulars waiting out in space for it and pack up the flier."

"How soon can your ships get here?"

"A couple of days at best, and they'll just about have to burn out their tubes to manage that." He gave an angry shake of his head. "They pulled back to watch another suspect planet nearby when I was sent here."

That had been a bad move, once again dictated by the Stellar Patrol's shortage of ships and manpower. The only truly close backup they had right now were the three tiny vessels on Sapphire. Those would have to be put on standby to intercept if necessary, but there was all-too-great a possibility one of the two pirates would make her escape.

If she carried even part of the various stolen chemicals, at least one poor world would suffer the consequences.

He shrugged. He would have to work around that handicap. Complaining about it now was useless and would only waste both time and energy. "I'll just have to see to it that I don't need help."

"Why not wait until reinforcements arrive and nab the sons and the whole cargo on-world?" she asked in alarm. Was he actually thinking of going up against those renegades alone, with no more to aid him than a civilian, a cam bull, and a nonmilitary flier?

"I'll wait if I can, but there may not be time. Until I assure myself otherwise, I'll have to assume I'm on my own and act accordingly." He gave her a tight smile. "I've had to do it before now, Banna."

The archopologist straightened. "You know what you will require from your own gear," she said decisively after a moment. "I will start pulling together the rest of our supplies and fueling the flier. We should start out as soon as you complete your transmissions."

"We?" he responded. "You're riding a comet's tail to the next galaxy if you imagine I'm going to expose you to what may become a firefight."

The woman braced herself. She had known the Ranger was not going to like this, but she was determined to have her will. "Put it on freeze, Taigue. Granted, I cannot fight and must stay out of that part of it, but I am coming with you. I can help with the driving, at least, and help manage the cam."

She met his gaze steadily. "Think, man. What am I to do here? Sit around shivering, not knowing whether it's you who will be coming back to me or a pack of space predators? Maybe I'll be waiting in vain, and no one will be returning. What if I find myself alone on Ruby of Diamond without even a flier to carry me back to a spaceport now run by the dead?" The black eyes locked with his, and there was no yielding in them. "Good or bad, I intend to know the outcome as it develops."

For several moments, Murchu remained firm in his refusal, but then his head lowered. Lis was right. Any failure or partial failure on his part could—no, almost certainly would—bring an attack down on her here in the ruin, and any rough camp outside it which they could establish in the time frame available to them would nearly as surely be discovered and destroyed. If Banna were with him, he could at least try to see to her defense. At the very least, his mind would stay more completely on the task before him if he was not squandering energy fretting over what might be taking place elsewhere.

"Very well," he told her gruffly. "You've been a help and no burden so far. I just hope you don't wind up paying a heavy price for your daring. Whether I live or die myself, I don't want that on my conscience."

Chapter Seventeen

Taigue scanned the deep pink expanse of the horizon, looking for any sign of another flier, or for any movement at all.

Banna Lis was keeping an equally close watch beside him, closer since she did not have the responsibility of the controls to claim her attention.

His expression softened as he glanced at her. Space, he thought, but she had strength. She might be correct in saying a citizen's duty forced her to aid him, but that carried only so far. The Auroran had no training to fit her for involvement in his work on this level. She had to be terrified—even he feared the flaming death they might encounter at any moment—yet she did not waver. Only her uncommon silence and the tense set of her face gave any indication she was aware of their potential peril at all.

His eyes closed. The Spirit of Space help him, but he did not want anything to happen to this woman. What he wanted . . .

A new fear struck him, trivial in the face of everything else looming over them and depending on them but choking all the same in its intensity. It was possible, even likely, one or both of them would die very shortly and that Banna Lis would never know what he had come to feel for her, what he only now recognized himself, although it had been awake within him for some time.

He could bear the thought of death but not that he should go to the Grim Commandant without ever having told her, without her ever realizing there was more in him than the instincts of a fighter and explorer.

"Banna, when I suggested having the joy of you back there, it was in jest."

The Auroran looked at him as if he had gone mad. "I think maybe I suspected as much, especially since I gave you the lead," she responded dryly.

"My interest is quite real, not just in knowing you, which I do want, but in having you with me long term." When recognition didn't light up Banna's eyes, Taigue, said, "Permanently."

A flush of anger colored her pale cheeks. "Are you mocking me?"

The Ranger recoiled. "I assure you, I'm quite serious."

"You, a Ranger who's a perfect specimen of a man, would want this?" She gestured to herself. "A widow who traipses about the galaxy digging in the rock with her hands in other people's memories?" She folded her arms. "I assure you, Taigue Murchu, there is no glory in my life that would attract you, nor in my appearance, so I'd thank you not to toy with my feelings."

Murchu raised his hands. "I'm in full truth. I am attracted to both your life and your appearance, and—"

She slammed her hand on the flyer controls. "You may be Patrol bred, but you are still basically prototypically Terran in your outlook. Do you imagine I am such as fool as to be unaware of how I measure beside your kind's physical ideal?"

"Damn my supposed ideal to every hell in the ultrasystem! A Patrol agent's not blind to other standards. You're beautiful, and you're Banna Lis. What more could any man worthy of the title desire?"

He stopped speaking, genuinely confused. "I don't fit your race's ideal, either. With three-plus enlistments behind me and considering the disadvantages of my career in general, I can't be anyone's ideal."

The woman's anger vanished. She laughed softly, although she could not quite keep the tremor out of it. She wanted this man so badly, badly enough that she had scarcely dared permit herself to acknowledge her desire, and here he was, owning a similar feeling for her, when she had believed he saw her only as a comrade, and a poor one at that.

"You will do well enough, my friend," she told him gently. "It is no fault of yours which made me flame at you." Her gloved fingers brushed his. "No woman enjoys knowing most of the ultrasystem views her as ugly. I suppose I am sensitive on the subject, especially with the man I happen to love."

Taigue looked at her in wonder, scarcely believing he was hearing her correctly, then his head lowered. For several moments, he was aware only of his relief, of how greatly he had feared the Auroran's rejection, but soon embarrassment began to build in him. Whatever his own desire, he had shown extremely poor judgment in speaking to her about this now. Had her feelings been otherwise, he would have put the archopologist in a difficult position. They had to live and work too closely together for that.

Murchu chuckled suddenly. "I seem to make a habit of skirting regulations when you are around, Doctor. A Stellar Patrol agent is forbidden to proposition a civilian for his personal satisfaction while engaged on an active mission."

Banna smiled. "I doubt this falls into that category. Besides, you will not always be on active duty, will you?"

Taigue raised his eyebrows. "I'll make damn sure I won't. Even so, I should have held my peace until this is all over."

She reached for his hand. "I might never have known then. We have this much at least, whatever happens."

The Ranger-Captain pulled her to him and guided her to him softly, slowly. Space knew she might pull back once she realized what he was doing, and she deserved that chance, but instead, she leaned toward him and tilted her face to his. He kissed her, letting the warmth of her lips permeate his heart, an oasis of heat on Ruby's cold expanse.

In the next moment, he reluctantly drew away from her. It was time he gave his attention back to the task of managing the flier, which he had almost unconsciously brought to a stop during the last part of their conversation. He was aware of a quiet happiness and a sense of peace new to him. It was not necessary to say more, not for now. Later, aye. Then they would have to talk, for anything they hoped to build between them would have to grow around their own complex lives. They must know for certain there was in truth something genuine with which they could work. Some, maybe too much, of what they were experiencing might be rooted in the extraordinary circumstances in which they found themselves, coupled, of course, with the real respect and liking they had for one another.

That was not likely, he decided almost immediately. They were not adolescents, either of them, to be netted by mere passion and illusion. He was sure of himself, sure what had come to life within him was sound, and he was sure of Banna Lis. They would be safe to move now . . .

He smiled, amused by his impatience. They could wait, allow their relationship time for testing and development, before leaping into it. Besides, they had no choice except to wait. Their vehicle would not fly itself, and they would have too much else to occupy them when they did set it down for any appreciable length of time. Grow careless now, and they could well have no time left for anything.

* * * *

The off-worlders made good time. With the flier in the air and the bull able to travel at a normal pace, they suffered no delay as they sped toward the spot where the animal had been abandoned.

They would reach it soon. Taigue had set an absolutely direct course for it, swerving only for rises so high he feared they would be skylined over too great a distance to risk cresting them. That straight course sliced better than three hours off their journey on top of the time won by the greater speed they were able to maintain.

The pair suffered no hardship on this journey. With the canopy firmly closed, the flier's Arctic-class heater kept them warmer than they would have been in their tent. Neither even wore an inner jacket while within the machine.

The Ranger enjoyed the snug comfort to the full, and it was with no sense of pleasure that he at last came to a stop at their goal.

The cam exhibited no joy at seeing the place, he noted. The bull had followed along behind the vehicle, responding to the tug on his halter willingly enough, but now he stood braced squarely on his powerful legs, his head held low, obviously sulky and ill-tempered.

"He is afraid of being left behind again, I suppose," Banna observed. "You may need help managing him."

"No. He'll be relieved of any worry on that score once we start moving again. No use in both of us perishing with the cold."

Murchu struggled into his inner jacket and fastened the outer one over it, then he pulled his mask over his face. He unlatched the canopy. "Here goes. –Keep well back. I don't want him to think you're driving him, or we could wind up going around in circles."

The Auroran's eyes narrowed. "I hope you are not planning on taking all the outside work yourself, Taigue Murchu. My feet are as sound as yours."

He shook his head. "I have to do it, Banna. I'll be scouting as well, looking for indications that we really are on the correct trail."

She bit her lip. She wanted to argue, knowing the punishment ahead of him, but he had her. She did not have the skill to take the task from him.

Taigue slid out of the machine, closing the door quickly behind him to conserve the heat inside.

He approached the cam warily, keeping out of range of his hooves. Picking up the lead chain, whose end he prudently left fastened to the flier in case the animal should bolt, he drew it back in the manner of a rein.

Immediately, the cam tried to turn back in the direction from which they had come. Taigue stopped him. The animal then started toward the port, but the Ranger again firmly checked the attempt. "Get on with you, you son. You know where to go."

The bull grunted and began moving due north.

Murchu waved at Banna and then quickened his pace to match that of their guide.

* * * *

The Ranger-Captain huddled inside his clothes and tried to ignore the savage, ceaseless clawing of the cold. There was no escape from it, no way to blunt its torture, and every step he took was a double battle, to move at all when he knew he had but to surrender and go back to the flier in order to find warmth and the even more difficult struggle to keep his mind on what he was doing.

It would have been a demanding enough job just to carry his role as a drover, for he had to provide sufficient presence to keep the cam moving without influencing the course he took, and he had to watch as well for any sign that others had passed this way before them.

Ruby's rugged, wind-swept surface did not aid such a search. There was no soil to pick up a hoof print, no vegetation to be broken or nibbled, and any gravel or small stone displaced by a heavily laden animal or one of those driving it was soon shifted again into some more natural position by the seemingly never-ending gale. After several fruitless, miserable miles, he began to fear he would discover no definite trail at all—or that there was no trail to be discovered, that their four-legged companion was not following any established route but had only set out according to his own incomprehensible fancy.

If they were going wrong, that much more precious time was lost to them, time they might not be able to recover later. People could die because of his mistake.

Suddenly, he saw something ahead, a small, dark mound standing out in sharp contrast to the rust-colored ground. He hurried toward it and knelt down. "The Spirit of Space be praised!"

Normally, he would be furious to find this on a planet as sterile as Ruby of Diamond, where the Settlement Board strictly demanded that latrine powder be used to eliminate off-world animal as well as human waste, but now he regarded it with relief.

The flier came to a stop beside him, and Banna opened the door a crack. "What have you discovered, Taigue?"

"Cam dung. We're on the right track."

"Thank Creation's Lord!"

"That's very nearly what I said."

The archopologist's eyes fixed on her companion, trying to penetrate his mask. She did not at all like the sound of his voice, even with the relief on him. Rangers, all Patrol agents, were a tough breed, accustomed to hardship, but they were still flesh and blood. There was also the chance Taigue might be pushing himself too hard rather than admit weakness in front of her.

No, she was wronging him. Murchu would never pull a vacuum-brained stunt like that with so much riding on him. From what she had seen of him, he was no such fool at any time. "Will you be able to ride now?" she pressed.

"Not for a while yet. I'll have to stay with the cam. He's used to a driver, apparently, and he could lose purpose without one, worse luck to him. Besides, I might just spot something else useful."

* * * *

That had not been the answer Taigue Murchu had wanted to make, but he resolutely set out again. Once he was dead certain they were on the pirates' trail, he might take it a bit easier, but for now, he had best resign himself to going on as he was.

He was rewarded by finding another deposit of cam scat and a few places where the gravel forming most of the surface in this region had been disturbed in a manner significant when taken with the rest, although each discovery would have been inconclusive by itself.

He turned his thoughts to those they were trying to trace. The space slime had been sly enough, he had to admit. It had been a good move to reserve their Arctic gear, which he now knew they must have, for use on the trail, thus making sure they would call no particular attention to themselves from anyone seeing them around the port.

That would have been the command of whomever had planned the robbery, the Ranger decided grimly, and it boded ill for his own cause. Foresight was to be expected, but he did not like at all the degree of control demonstrated by the enforcing of such an order on the undisciplined crews he had seen on a world with a climate like Ruby's.

Murchu liked even less that those spacers had been induced to make several journeys of more than a day's duration each across the planet's inhospitable surface, utilizing unfamiliar, unpleasant animals as beasts of burden instead of doing it all in a few quick, relatively easy trips in a heated flier.

More than the desire to save fuel had moved them, of course. A flier ran the risk of being spotted, and its presence in the wild questioned, by either the Stellar Patrol or by Settlement Board personnel. Both of those came to Ruby unannounced and could not merely be eliminated without inviting even greater official interference.

Be that as it might, pirates were not fond of inconvenience, and the fact that they had stuck it out, aye, and had repeatedly exposed themselves to the really acute discomfort they would have encountered here was a dark omen for some site or sites elsewhere in the ultrasystem. The payment would have to be rich and sure to secure the kind of co-operation these raiders had given, and the ultimate reward would be immeasurably greater still for the masterminds.

Murchu's eyes closed. The threat posed by the supplies taken in the Gamma of Chadwick robbery could not be underestimated, nor could the urgency of the situation in which he found himself on Ruby of Diamond. So much was riding on him. Too much. If he failed, the guilt for the lives he had not shielded from slaughter and ruin would be with him for whatever remained to him of existence.

Chapter Eighteen

Once again, late in the day, Murchu called a halt. This was a more important find than the others had been, the definite remains of a campsite, one which had been occupied on several separate occasions.

Guiltily occupied. An effort had been made to conceal the marks of human intrusion into the sheltered pocket which had shielded the encampment from both wind and unwelcome observation. It was a good attempt and would have thrown off any of the pirates' own kind, but the space hounds' on-world skills were not sufficient to baffle a veteran agent of the Exploratory Force.

Taigue at last allowed himself the luxury of rejoining his companion in the flier. "The spaceport's about a full day's cam trek from here," he told her with satisfaction. "I'd say our opponents used to break their journey here and then go on, maybe for another complete day, maybe part of a day, to their depot."

"It sound's reasonable, but there might also be a great deal more than a single day's travel still to go."

"Hardly. They'd never have used the cams in that case. Even this much of a journey is pushing probability. Time considerations aside, it's not easy putting up with Ruby's climate."

Banna was watching the Ranger closely as she was listening. He was slumped against the seat as if completely spent, and he was shivering violently despite his heavy clothing and the heat inside the vehicle. It was apparent, at least to her, that he would not be able to continue much longer as he had been going.

"I do not like your having to put up with it yourself, Taigue," she said seriously. "You are risking real cold injury, and what use will you be to anyone if you let yourself get crippled at this stage?"

He smiled. "I've been monitoring myself for that, but you can stop worrying. I'm withdrawing from exterior service, for the time being anyway. Our bull should keep going on his own from this point. The stockpile's the closest shelter he knows."

"We will camp here?"

Murchu shook his head. "No, not here. We can't chance having a party of those renegades dropping in on us unexpectedly, unlikely as that may be. We'll continue on until close to nightfall and stop then. That is not far off, and we'll have made a start on tomorrow's journey."

He fumbled with his mask and finally succeeded in drawing it off over his head, but the cold had gone through him, and he did not want to remove his gloves or outer jacket.

The archopologist was having no part of that. She did not entirely trust his assurances of well-being, and she wanted to confirm for herself that he was all right.

She was well familiar with the fastenings of the gloves and soon had them off. "Oh, Taigue!"

He glanced at his hands. There was no damage, but they were an ugly purple-red which proclaimed he had not been far from it. They also hurt abominably. "They're sound out, more or less. I wouldn't have let it go any farther."

"Naturally not," she snapped. "What about your feet?"

"Not nearly as bad."

"Numb?"

"Throbbing like a spacer's hell. Nothing wrong with the circulation in either of them."

Banna held his hands between hers trying to force her own warmth into them. She released him after a while. She had brought a canteen of strong jakek with her and had set it on her plutonium disk as soon as she had seen her companion heading for the flier. It was now steaming hot and should go far in setting him to rights.

His brows raised when she handed it to him. "Did I ever mention that you'd be an asset to a Ranger team, Doctor?"

Her eyes danced. "No, though you have occasionally rather grudgingly hinted as much."

Murchu drank slowly, savoring the jakek's rich flavor. The hot liquid was already establishing a core of warmth within him that would soon banish the remaining tendrils left by the cold. In the meantime, he could sit back and relax. He knew there was no point in trying to argue the archopologist into turning the controls over to him. He did not feel particularly up to taking them anyway, and so he decided to capitulate gracefully and enjoy the rest. It would only be for another hour or two at the most. After that, the cam would be tiring for a fact, and it would have grown too dark to keep a proper eye on the course they were following.

* * * *

They continued for another hour and a half before the woman brought the flier to a halt. "Here, Taigue? I do not think we can see well enough to go on."

He roused himself out of the near doze into which he had fallen and gave a quick look at the campsite she had selected. He nodded in appreciation. Lis had set down in the midst of a cluster of stones, a formation similar to the one used by the pirates they were tracking. They would have shelter from the wind here and also from chance observation by any others ranging Ruby's frigid desert.

"I couldn't have chosen better myself."

The Ranger drew on his outer jacket. He did not fancy facing the cold again, but he had somewhat accustomed himself to it at least and might as well finish up the day's chores. There was no point in sending Banna out there as well.

First, he fed and watered the cam. The big animal swallowed his portion quickly, without seeming to chew or draw breath, then he lay down, settling himself between two tall, flat rocks with a grunt of contentment.

Taigue watched him half enviously. The bull was obviously quite oblivious to the biting temperature, and now that his belly was reasonably full, he appeared as much at ease as the humans were in their flier.

Murchu left him to examine their campsite more closely. It was fascinating in itself, as were all such formations on Ruby's broken surface, and he wished for the thousandth time that he could explore the planet properly. He would have loved to delve into this particular place, try to discover its precise history, to piece together the sequence of events which had led to its present form.

He wished he were able to record this world's stark beauty. He had a small talent with sketching pencil and paint, and there was that inside him which ached to capture Ruby of Diamond.

The Ranger-Captain shook his head sadly. He only rarely had that kind of time for himself. Of a certainty, he did not have it on this assignment.

He scanned the horizon with practiced care, although he did not anticipate discovering any sign of their foes. The sky was dusky now in Diamond's last rays. It reminded him of congealing blood. He had seen that too often in his career, he thought grimly.

He had seen it as a cadet years ago on Tatarina. A rush of fear swept through him. The cause would be different this time, but he dreaded having to look upon a similar massacre again, perhaps repeated on several different planets.

Dwelling on horror would not avert it. Murchu turned his mind from the shadow looming over the unknown targets the pirates' employers had chosen for their victims and forced it back to the sky itself.

He frowned. Normally a planet's idiosyncrasies did not trouble him even when he did not care for them, but that pink firmament played on his nerves. His dislike would not interfere with his ability to work, but he would never feel comfortable under it.

He wondered momentarily how the archopologist responded to seeing it for weeks on end but quickly decided it probably did not bother her at all. Banna's people liked comfort and civilized quarters, but they well-nigh fed on exotic surroundings. They were as a race jaded by what they regarded as the commonplace after so great an expanse of time, even a commonplace as lovely as Aurora provided.

Taigue started walking back toward the flier, moving briskly to warm himself. His kind regarded that love of distraction as a weakness, a sign of degeneration, but he could not see it had harmed his companion. Besides, was an Auroran's desire for the strange so different at its core from a Ranger's eagerness to explore a new planet or a settler's joy in intimately learning the ways of his adopted homeworld? Their performance in the War should be proof enough that all the citizens of the inner system needed was a chance to meet a real challenge for their inner strength to reassert themselves. With the chance to stretch into an unproductive field, new and unexpected strengths would rise up within them.

He bounded inside the vehicle and gratefully slammed the door shut beside him. "All nice and quiet," he reported."

"Good. We can use the peace. We will both be the better for having a proper rest."

Lis had readied their supper while he had been outside and handed him his share once he removed his outer garments. He turned to his plate without delay. Seafood tonight. The Ranger did not have to force himself to eat it. Exercise and low temperatures combined to produce a ravenous appetite.

He did appreciate the value of these rations and was genuinely grateful for them, however tiresome they could become with long-term use. They not only provided all the nutrients the body required, but they satisfied the stomach's craving for bulk. That was more than could be said for the old-time issue, which was strictly emergency fodder. He had been forced to survive on such supplies for a week following a crash into Loren's swamps, and his recollections of those days were decidedly unhappy. The old-style rations had sustained his health, right enough, but they had done nothing to assuage the pangs of hunger. That, at least, was no longer a problem.

Banna had neither done as much nor endured as much and so ate with less gusto, but she did not take much longer to clear her plate. When she had finished with it, she set it aside, reaching over the back of the seat to put it down in the cargo area behind them to await later attention. That done, she leaned back and closed her eyes. "It has been a long day."

"Aye, but fortunately not too eventful a one."

The man put his arm around her. He kissed her softly, then he closed her in a more demanding embrace.

She met his ardor with equal warmth, and his desire for her grew in force and urgency.

Suddenly, a warning sounded within him, the instinct born of a life-time spent in too close association with danger, and he reluctantly drew back. They dared not give themselves over like this.

Banna's black eyes opened. She realized what held him, and she gave him a rueful smile. "A Ranger never gets to go off duty?"

"Not when on an active assignment."

He kissed her again, tenderly, almost without regret. "We'll have time for the rest," he promised."

"Time in plenty."

So they would, the Auroran thought, and it would be the proper time, after they had pledged to one another before a priest of her people and before a priest of his as well. Most of Terra's stock had steadied in their old faiths once science had matured out of its unpleasant adolescence, and they had remained steady in those beliefs throughout the centuries of interstellar exploration and colonization. That, she recalled, was particularly true of Taigue's subrace with their long history of trial and struggle.

She glanced at him briefly, wondering if she would be able to match with such a man, if she had a right to attempt it. Aurora's settlement had been accomplished easily, or relatively easily. His history and his life were both filled with challenge.

Banna gripped herself. So, too, was her life. She need not feel ashamed of it, and because of all she had learned during its course, she could comprehend well enough what moved him. They would have to adapt to each other, certainly, but neither of them was a child. They would work together to make their marriage all such a relationship could be.

A deep contentment filled her. Taigue Murchu was worth that effort on her part. He was worth everything she could give, and while life remained in her, she would continue to give and to strive for his sake and for her own.

Chapter Nineteen

The Ranger-Captain looked down at his companion, at the little circle of her face visible through the opening she had left in the hood flap of her sleeping bag. She was pale, so wan that the blue lacing of veins stood out in stark relief. He hated the thought of waking her when he knew she was not nearly slept out, but Banna was right. They had to function as much as possible like full comrades. If he tried to spare her too much, he would end by weakening himself. They could not afford to be reckless with their resources, material or physical.

He smiled suddenly. He could not claim much greater holding power. He had dropped off last night before he had finished fastening his sleeping bag.

Taigue laughed softly at himself. It was a good thing for his pride that they had needed to keep a formal watch and forgo the fulfillment of their desire. He would have been decidedly embarrassed to have a woman like Banna Lis consent to warm his bed and then drop off like a grandfather in the days before medicine had at last eliminated the decay of senescence.

His fingers brushed her cheek. "Rise and shine, Doctor. Breakfast's ready."

One thing about her, she woke instantly and completely with no show of temper, although she would patently have preferred to stay where she was. A good many Rangers he knew had never quite managed the last part of that scenario.

"Morning so soon?" she asked. The world around seemed scarcely lighter than it had been at midnight.

"Predawn," he told her. "Diamond should be showing up by the time we're ready to go. I don't want to lose any of the daylight."

"Fair enough."

The archopologist accepted the plate he handed her, but she eyed the gloves on his lap disapprovingly. "I am really not going to allow you to keep on taking all the outside work. Granted, you have to scout, but I can jolly well feed the cam."

"I might as well do it again this morning. I want to muzzle him before we start out. He might get excited when we near the stockpile."

She nodded. One bellow like the bull gave when he had scented them at the wrong moment, and they had both booked passage on their last voyage.

The Auroran did not offer further protest. She would have done the job had it been necessary or if Taigue had asked her, but she was as happy not having to work so closely with the irritable creature.

Her expression clouded for a moment. "You will be careful?"

"You can put credits down on that. As sure as space is black, I don't want another sample of his temper."

That, he did not. He was still damn sore after his first dose, and he approached the bull cautiously. The animal was well trained, however, and accustomed to the discipline of the trail, and once he had eaten, he accepted the man's handling, even the unfamiliar muzzle, without protest.

* * * *

They made even better time than they had on the previous day. The cam was extending himself, moving with steady, smooth strides that whittled the miles away seemingly without effort. It was plain to both off-worlders that the big creature had some goal in mind, although they were somewhat surprised by his apparent eagerness to reach it."

Taigue puzzled over that for a while, then dismissed the matter. The animals were probably customarily granted an extended rest at the end of their journey, that and a good feeding and watering. Their guide would be anticipating a similar break at the end of this jaunt.

He turned his attention to the country around them. It was changing in nature as they moved away from the riverbed, growing more rugged, with an ever-increasing number of huge boulders and jagged rises, incredibly sharp and twisted formations that seemed something born of a god's nightmare.

The ground beneath them altered in nature as well. The eternal ruddy color remained, but they no longer encountered so much of the solid rock and lava they had found earlier. Here, their footing consisted of a great deal of broken stone, boulders of every size, and gravel, all but the largest pieces showing signs of frequent disturbance by the vicious winds. There were even odd patches of coarse sand lodged in a very few highly sheltered pockets, the first appreciable quantity he had seen.

That might be all of it which was visible, but there was plenty of small, loose stuff flying around. The sharp little grains seemed to strike at his eyes of their own accord if he left himself unprotected for any length of time, and the Ranger quickly learned to don goggles as well as his mask whenever he ventured outside.

He did not do so often. He gave his trust to the cam that day and left the vehicle only every now and then to check their course. There was no point in punishing himself. The chance of any kind of a trail's surviving for more than a few hours in this endlessly changing terrain was infinitesimally small. Occasional spot checking in places of some potential would suffice.

* * * *

Taigue returned to his seat after yet another fruitless expedition. "I hope that demon knows where he's going," he grumbled.

"You cannot be making dramatic discoveries all the time," the woman reasoned calmly. "Just sit back and relax, Captain. It is obvious he has been this way before."

No, there was no questioning that. The beast had a real purpose to his march, and its end was not terribly far off, either, not if speed was any indication. The bull had increased his pace until he was moving at a rhythmic half lope that the humans would have been hard pressed to match had they been forced to go on foot.

Murchu turned to the Auroran. "I don't know when we're going to reach the stockpile or how fast things will start to happen once we do, but I want you to be ready to grab your pack and run as soon as I give the word. Both of us will. We'll probably split up shortly after we're outside. You go to ground, and I'll see what havoc I can manage to create."

"What about the flier?"

"Leave it. If I get into trouble, the raiders will assume I had transport and may come looking for it if they . . . gain the advantage, but they're not likely to imagine I've brought company along. I'll come back for you when I can."

"If you can't?" she asked as she slipped on her pack.

"You'll be on your own then. You'll just have to pray they don't find the flier. In any event," he added sternly, "keep away from their camp. You won't be able to help me, and you might cause trouble for both of us."

The woman accepted his command quietly, or seemed to accept it. She would obey him while Murchu made his approach, she decided in her own mind, and during any active battle, which would be clearly audible, but if he did not come back after a reasonable time, then she would go seeking him. Returning to the ruins alone would do her no good, even in the unlikely event she could make it back by herself with or without the vehicle. That space scum would strike there as a matter of course almost as soon as they finished off her companion. She would be as well off following her inclination and doing whatever she could to aid him as she would by retiring and waiting to be butchered like a beast in its lair.

* * * *

The off-worlders lowered the setting on the heater as they began to feel the effects of their heavy gear, but neither thought to remove or even loosen their clothing. The cam's open impatience communicated itself to them, and early as it was in the day, they felt with increasing certainty that the end of their journey was not far off. Both made sure their blasters rested in easy reach of their hands, and Murchu's eyes were never still as he scanned the sky and horizon and the world around them.

There was little conversation between the pair as they strained to catch any alien sound, anything that was not the soughing of the wind or the softer hum of their own passage.

Three-quarters of an hour passed peacefully, as had all the hours before, then, with breathless suddenness, the lifeless rhythm of the desert planet was shattered by an eerie, prolonged wail.

Taigue's heart leaped but in the next moment steadied as he recognized the sound. A cam. The animal was still distant, probably a mile or more off although it was difficult to judge precisely, but it was more than near enough for it to have scented or sensed their presence or that of their guide.

Quick as he had been to identify the source of the disturbance, the cam bull responded more rapidly still. He plunged ahead so abruptly and with such force that he jerked the flier forward, whipping it out of the man's control.

Murchu fought to regain command of the machine before it could slam into one of the stone teeth forever gnashing at Ruby's flushed sky.

For several minutes, he struggled merely to avoid collision, driving as if he were on a professional obstacle course, twisting and spinning in such tight maneuvers that he began to fear the civilian craft would not be able to withstand the stress.

In the end, he felt the vehicle respond to him again. Once he was sure of his control, he used the flier's weight and the strength of its engine to bring the cam back to heel once more.

The Ranger did not so much as give himself time to draw a steadying breath. He set down in the best shelter he could find near at hand, a sharply sloping wall of rock which formed a deep, probably perpetual shadow at its base. No sooner had the flier touched the ground and ceased moving than he deactivated the engine and threw open the door. Catching Banna's arm with one hand and his pack with the other, he leaped outside.

"Run! We have to put distance between ourselves and this thing."

There wasn't even time to unhook the cam from the flyer. Flee they did, keeping low as they raced over the broken ground, holding as much as possible to cover and crossing more open spots in quick, lung-bursting spurts.

At last, they cast themselves into a pool of frigid shade thrown by yet another low cliff a good quarter of a mile from the place from which they had started.

All the while, the strange cam continued to call at intervals of several seconds, but there appeared to be no response from the still-invisible camp. Five minutes passed. Ten. Still nothing.

The Ranger-Captain raised himself a little from the ground where he lay sprawled. "Stay here," he commanded in a whisper. "I'll go on to the base."

Banna Lis nodded numbly. Tears filled her eyes as she watched him move out, cautiously now, more Commando than Patrol agent. Her gloved hands dug convulsively into the ground beneath her. Creation's Lord, but she loved him, and she might never again see him alive.

* * * *

Murchu crept forward, striving to put a good distance between himself and their hiding place as quickly as possible lest by some cruel twist of chance, his movements should draw their enemies' attention to his companion.

It went against every desire inside him to leave the Auroran woman alone and frightened in this frigid waste, but he had no acceptable alternative. He had to do this—he had been sent to Ruby of Diamond to do it—and, surprisingly capable as Lis had proven herself during their recent dash, she did not have the training to accompany him farther, not under Diamond's full light.

His own skill might not be sufficient. Any slip, any frown from fortune, could betray him with almost certainly fatal result to him and to his cause.

Taigue shuddered in his heart. He had always respected death, but for the first time, the thought of dying filled him with dread. He would indeed be abandoning Banna then, and he knew full well it would be to a slower and crueler doom than he would face. He had no illusions about her chances of permanently eluding those renegades once they were alerted to their danger.

Another blast of fear ripped through him, baser but natural enough that he did not condemn it or himself for harboring it at such a moment. For the first time since he had been a very young man, he had the promise of a richness in his life extending beyond the satisfaction and importance of his work, the hope of a new happiness and personal closeness both fate and he himself had previously denied. He dreaded and resented that all of it might be stripped from him again before it had so much as come into true bud.

The man gripped his thoughts. He would kill them both for a fact if he did not keep a better hold than this on himself. There was a task before him, one demanding the whole of his attention. Other thoughts, other concerns, even consciousness of the awesome responsibility he was carrying, all that had to be forgotten until he had seen this through to its end.

The loose surface was not easy to cross silently or without creating a trail which would stand out like a beacon from the air, but he had managed to maneuver in worse country, to his quarry's ultimate sorrow. The Ranger utilized the full of his skill now. He was blessed with satisfactory cover along most of the way and so made surprisingly good time despite the fact that he dared not come to his feet at all.

The cold was ever present, but the low profile he maintained made him a poor target for the wind, and the effort he had to put forth in his uncomfortable advance warmed him so he suffered less than might otherwise have been the case had his way been easier.

Airborne debris gave him the most trouble. The wind was higher today than he had previously encountered on Ruby, and it was carrying a load of small particles, driving them with force enough that he could feel the blow of the larger pieces whenever they struck against his mask. He would have been hard put to go on at all without the goggles protecting his eyes.

Murchu came upon the camp quite suddenly, almost literally crawling into it. He stopped short, flattening as he did so and tensing instinctively to receive the blaster bolt he more than half expected.

In the next moment, he raised his head slightly. The life seemed to wither inside him as he surveyed the scene in front of him.

* * * *

Banna Lis clenched her teeth to keep them from chattering uncontrollably. Tremor after tremor wrenched through her body as the chill bit deeply into her. Ruby of Diamond was no world for lying out still and exposed for prolonged stretches at a time.

It was not only the cold that was setting her shaking. Terror had its part in it, for herself, for Taigue, for those unknown people whose future was hanging on their actions here.

How was the Ranger-Captain faring? It seemed so long since he had left her, but she knew it would take time just to reach the pirates' encampment, much less to plan and then carry out an attack on them.

She should know when the last was in progress, at least. Surely, there would be noise or the flash of blasters or, hopefully, roaring flames turning Ruby's sky ghastly as the cargo went up. Unless Murchu failed . . .

The Auroran's hands gripped her blaster. She was realistic about her probable future in that event. If the raiders found her, she knew there would be no altering her fate, but she had taught herself to use one of these things more than passing well. Humans might not be the same as lifeless targets, but the vermin she would be facing could scarcely be termed that, and she was determined to take out one or maybe more of her assailants before they burned her down. That much she owed to herself and to Taigue Murchu.

A movement, the sound of a booted foot striking gravel in front of and to her right!

Nerving herself, Lis sighted her weapon in its direction, slowly drawing the trigger back. The safety was already off, and the fire setting was at broad beam to slay.

"Banna?"

She lowered the blaster with a sigh of relief at the soft call. "Taigue! Praise the Spirit ruling Space."

She was pleased he had shown enough respect for her that he had not just risen up suddenly in front of her seemingly from out of the ground.

The Ranger gave a nod of approval for the way she had held her weapon when he did stand but then strode over to her and gave his hand to help raise her.

"We're too late," he told her grimly. "They've already taken the cargo."

Chapter Twenty

The archopologist felt what little color the cold had left her drain beneath her mask. "When?" she heard herself ask.

"Last night as nearly as I can determine. We only missed them by that much."

"But the cam?"

"Abandoned like ours was. They'd apparently been moving the stuff when we planeted, which is why we never saw all of them. Those out here probably received a transmission from the spaceport to stay put until we were supposedly safe at the ruins, then their flier came here and took the remainder of their goods off, traveling at night to avoid any odd chance of our spotting them and mentioning their presence when you checked in with Sapphire."

"So they are gone—" She sounded and was numb.

"Maybe not. I'm thinking they won't lift until tonight, maybe around dawn. They're at a crucial stage now and won't be taking needless risks with off-worlders. They don't doubt the Patrol's intelligence, and even one word of warning could bring a galaxy of trouble on them. As a precaution, they'll almost certainly have stashed their cargo in that second warehouse, the one they supposedly were not using, so they can claim complete ignorance in the event of a major search. They'll load their fighters after dark when all crates look pretty much the same to a casual onlooker."

"Maybe the buyers will send a freighter to collect everything," Lis suggested.

Taigue shook his head. "Not on-world. They're too smart to come anywhere near Diamond's system. The contraband will either be transferred in space a safe distance from prying Patrol eyes or else delivered to some prearranged site as I've believed from the beginning."

"Do we still have a chance to stop them?" Murchu seemed to believe they did from what he said earlier.

"If I have anything to do with it, we do. —You must stay here—"

"Put that debris on freeze!" the woman snapped. "What are we going to do?"

"Go back for the flier first and bring our cam to the camp. We'll tie him with the cow." He scowled unconsciously. "I did delay long enough to feed and water her. The raiders left the animals' supplies after them as well, though not where the poor things could reach any of them."

The Auroran's eyes darkened. "What will happen to them if we are killed?"

"They'll be the first of many innocent victims, more innocent than most of those to follow. Raklik is illegal for excellent reason, and the ones it kills will have chosen to use it." He glanced back in the direction of the abandoned base. "I can't do more for them, Banna," he told her quietly. "We'll have to make real speed now, whatever chance we have of accomplishing anything."

Lis bit her lip. "I am sorry, Taigue. I was thinking like a civilian."

"It's my fault you have to think any other way," Murchu responded bitterly.

Without another word, he started walking briskly in the direction of their vehicle.

The archopologist ran a few steps to catch up with him. "It really is all on us, is it not?"

"I'm afraid so. It would take a miracle for reinforcements to arrive here in time to stop those fighters once they lift."

"What about the ships on Sapphire?" The Ranger had said before that he did not believe they could prevent the renegades' escape. "Three of ours to the renegades' two."

"They'll try," her companion said wearily, "but I doubt they'll blow both fugitives. Pirates fight too well, and our people will be out-classed." He sighed. That dismissal seemed an injustice to the agents manning the Stellar Patrol craft. Regulars were accustomed to battle in space and were as good as any soldiers the Navy produced. "We have only two-man splinters," he explained. "They'll be at a major disad-vantage facing a brace of five-class raider fighters armed to the prover-bial teeth. It's doubtful they'll be able to take out both pirates, and the two of them must be destroyed, or we'll have failed. As it is, even if we destroy their plans, only a direct gift from the Spirit of Space Himself will give us the masterminds of all this. They'll go free, losing no more than the credits they've spent."

He fell silent again, but he frowned and his head lifted after he had gone a couple of yards. He slowed nearly to a stop. "What's the time Banna? It can't be late enough for the sky to be that dusky."

The archopologist's brows came together for a moment, then her hand went to her mouth. "Space! The Great Creator help us! Taigue, a sandstorm, and it is on top of us."

The off-worlders started to run, covering ground at a fast, hard gal-lop spurred by fear. Murchu might not know what it meant on this part of Ruby, but he was well acquainted with the havoc such tempests cre-ated on other worlds, and the woman's reaction was goad enough. She was not one to panic at shadows. If there was no sea of sand here to roll down on top of them, gravel and small stones could act the part of mis-siles with the same deadly effect if driven by a sufficiently powerful wind.

The gale struck the pair like a blow from a titanic fist. It rocked them both, but they regained their balance and continued driving against it, keeping their heads low to guard their masks against its full blast. If those should be shredded, the flesh of their faces would not be long in following.

They gained two hundred yards. The wind veered without warning, sweeping around and striking them from the side with a renewed force that threw Banna to the ground.

The man had enough additional weight to hold him on his feet this time, but despair filled him. They did not have a hope of reaching the flier. The tempest was gaining strength with each passing second. He would not be able to keep going long more against it, and Lis obviously could not continue at all.

Their clothes would not hold up, either. Already, there were several rents in both his jacket and his trousers, and his left arm was numb after a glancing blow he had taken from a stone more than large enough to break the limb—or his head—had it struck directly.

He caught his companion's arm and hauled her to her feet, then propelled her toward a stand of roughly rectangular stone blocks to their left.

Staggering under the battering of the wind, Taigue forced himself onward until he reached a point most closely resembling a lea in the chaos screaming around them.

"Down!"

He knew the Auroran could not hear him over the tumult howling around them, but he pushed her to the ground. He threw himself on top of her, hoping to shield her, at least, even if he himself were to be pummeled to death.

The Ranger-Captain hunched his shoulders to give his neck as much protection as he could and pressed his face against Banna's shoulder.

After that, he could only endure. There was little real sand to drift on top of them, and getting down to ground level took them beneath much of the wind's fury. The big rocks above and around helped even more, breaking the force of the gale and deflecting much of the debris it carried, but despite their shielding, Taigue could feel the constant pelting of hard particles against his back, and several times, he jerked involuntarily as fist-sized stones drove into his back and legs.

The punishment continued for twenty minutes longer, and then the air grew perceptibly quieter. As it stilled, its burden of flying material dropped to nearly normal level.

The man shifted slightly, slowly testing himself. He appeared to have escaped real injury, but after having locked his muscles so tightly for that length of time, he felt as stiff and sore as if he had taken a beating.

His throat closed. There was no move out of Banna. If she was dead, then his own survival meant nothing. Even those strangers he was striving to save meant nothing.

The fear left him again. It was groundless. The archopologist was stirring now. He should have realized full well that she was safe. Nothing, or very little, had touched her, and he had felt the warmth of her body and the rhythm of her breathing during the whole of it to assure him of her well-being.

Murchu forced himself to relax. He had been an utter vacuum brain, and he was extremely grateful he had not betrayed his unfounded panic, but chiefly, he wondered at the intensity of it. How could anyone have become everything to a man in so short a span of time?

Banna Lis' eyes fixed on him. She had felt him wince when each of the larger stones had struck him and could only guess how many times he had been able to suppress his reaction to similar or lesser blows.

A few moments' observation told her that he seemed to have escaped significant hurt, but the backs of both his jacket and trouser legs were badly rent. He would be in a pity from the cold before they reached the flier.

Her lips tightened. There was nothing she could do to help him. Even if she herself could survive without her outer gear. Taigue Murchu would accept no such offering from her. He would have to go on as best he could until they gained their flier.

What would they find when they did arrive at its hiding place? There should be little to fear with respect to the vehicle itself. It was a sturdy machine, and it would have enjoyed great shelter where they had left it, far better than they had known. Only by the most malignant chance would it have suffered more than superficial damage. It was the fate of the unfortunate bull that concerned her.

"I wonder how our poor cam fared?" she ventured sadly."

"Probably pretty well," the Ranger responded, speaking only slightly more hopefully than he actually felt. "His ancestors were desert bred, and the old survival instincts and abilities should still be in him. He's not all that different from them physically." He straightened. "Good or ill, we'll learn his fate soon enough."

* * * *

The pair moved quickly, but even had they run the whole distance, they could not have gone fast enough for Taigue Murchu. His torn clothing seemed to afford him no protection whatsoever. The cold was not merely unpleasant now but a torture, a torment that made all the previous discomfort he had endured on Ruby of Diamond stand as nothing beside it. There was no release from it, nothing at all he could do to lessen it. He could only try to endure and hope he would reach shelter before he took irreparable injury, as he knew he must very soon.

* * * *

Taigue realized they had only a short way left to go, that the place where they had left the flier was near, but it was solely by the lash of his will that he managed to force himself to cover the final few hundred feet. Death, any death, whether the slow, strange sleep cold eventually brought or a blaster's fast, searing oblivion, seemed infinitely preferable to continuing longer in this agony. He wished his body would go numb despite the evil that portended, anything to end his pain.

Once they actually sighted their goal, his mind snapped clear of the fog in which he had been moving. Whatever his misery and his desire to have it end, his training held, and he approached the concealed machine cautiously, signaling Banna to remain where she was.

After a few moments, he chuckled and called for her to join him. "Look at our friend. You wasted your sympathy on him at any rate."

The cam had forced his way between the rock and the flier and had lain down there with his back to the storm. Scarcely any wind at all would have been able to come at him directly. He had been asleep in point of fact and only shuffled to his feet at the sound of the man's voice.

Murchu rubbed his nose. "Here, old fellow. Let's get rid of this muzzle. There's no point in keeping it on you now. Have a chat with your lady friend if you'd like."

No sooner had he removed improvised silencer than the bull gave a long, undulating bellow. It was answered in the next moment by the distant cow.

"It sounds as if she weathered the storm as well," Banna said with relief.

"I figured she would. I put her where she could get into shelter, where the cargo was stored as a matter of fact." He patted their charge's neck. "Feed and water him, will you, while I check out the flier?"

"My pleasure, Captain." The black eyes ranged over him. "Fetch a sleeping bag out of there and pull it over your shoulders before you start. You will be in trouble otherwise. We cannot afford that."

The Ranger-Captain gave her a mock salute but was quick to obey.

He sat inside for a few seconds after settling the bag around himself, waiting for his body to warm a little before facing the outer world again. Although there was no heat on, it was so good merely to be free of the bone-penetrating wind that he could have wept for relief, and he had to will himself to leave the shelter again.

Murchu was not kept outside for long. As he had believed would prove the case, the flier had come through the sandstorm nearly unscathed, although it could have suffered badly had it enjoyed less cover. A considerable amount of paint was gone from its exposed side There were several deep scratches gouged in the tough material of the canopy, but not enough to impair visibility through it. Neither was the engine fouled, though there had been little real danger of that last since the tempest had carried only a small amount of material minute enough to work its way into the drive mechanism, shielded as it had been by the defenses of its location.

* * * *

They were not long in returning to the clearing the pirates had used for their clandestine storehouse.

The archopologist looked around, weighing the site with the eye of one well accustomed to selecting long-term camp grounds.

Nature had been kinder to the subbiotics than they or any like them deserved. The place was perfect for the purpose to which they had put it. Basically, it consisted of a jagged, roughly crescent-shaped cliff some one hundred fifty feet high. Cradled and sheltered between its arms was a dead level field of solid lava. Near the cliff's center, at its base, was a fairly long, shallow cave further protected from both the elements and aerial observation by a massive ledge shading its mouth. It was in there they had stored their contraband.

The roof was high enough for it to serve as a stable for the cams. Taigue fastened the bull to a rock close to its entrance, the same one restraining the cow. Their leads were long enough to allow them the choice of remaining outside or seeking the greater shelter of the cave.

Once he had assured himself both were secure and had full access to food and water, he rubbed their necks and returned to his vehicle with a heavy heart. It was not easy leaving living creatures like this, not knowing if he would be coming back or if he was abandoning them to a slow and hard death.

Banna made no protest as she walked away from them, but her mouth was trembling, and when she stole a last look at the cams, they seemed to gaze sadly and accusingly at her, as if they understood full well how uncertain their future was.

She squared her shoulders and quickened her pace. Taigue needed strength from her, not a show of grief over a situation neither of them could change. He was feeling badly enough about it himself to judge by the lingering caress he had given each of the animals and his lowered head when he had quit them after securing their bonds.

She swung into her place beside him. They should be back here soon. If they were not, well, there would be no guilt on them. They would be beyond mortal help themselves.

Chapter Twenty-One

The Ranger-Captain waited for his companion to settle herself. "I hope your nerves are good. I'm going to be letting this thing out, and we'll have to stay low."

"Have at it, friend. I copiloted Anna on Aurora's obstacle speed tracks in our misspent youth."

The archopologist was not so certain of the accuracy of her assurance a few seconds later when the speed gage shot to maximum and the altimeter showed them to be scarcely airborne at all. She bit her lip to stop herself from gasping and forced herself to keep her eyes open, but she could not draw her attention away from the instruments. Any error whatsoever on her companion's part, and fragments of them and their vehicle would be scattered for yards over this rusty waste.

Banna took a deep breath and made herself hold it. Taigue Murchu had shown himself to be anything but suicidal, and he was too filled with the sense of duty and the responsibility he carried to risk himself inordinately with a major mission before him. He would not be flying like this if he were not well able to handle it.

After that, she relaxed. She had always liked speed, and gradually she began to give herself over to the motion of the machine, in the end thoroughly enjoying the pace which had terrified her only a short time before.

Murchu spared her a glance to see how she was faring and received something of a surprise. The shooting star was having a good time. If he had been in her place, he would have been shivering where he sat.

He dared not divert more of his attention from what he was doing, and so he said nothing to her, not then or for the next several hours.

The Auroran remained still through most of that time, sitting more like a statue than a living being, but in the end, she fetched her plutonium disk from its place in her pack and two packets of rations along with it. When she had finished heating these, she ate her portion and then broke the long silence. "It is time I spelled you. Switch places with me now and eat this while it is hot. This stuff is abominable when it is cold."

The Ranger set the flier down without argument. One could keep going like this only so long before concentration and reaction time weakened. He would serve both of them and their cause by taking a break before that happened.

"Keep higher and go slower," he advised as he bit into his food. "The Patrol spent a long time teaching me to fly fast in poor conditions."

She laughed. "Never fear, Captain. Life is sweet to me, too."

The speed at which she started out belied her words. It was less than he had maintained, and their altitude was greater, but Taigue stopped eating and watched her uneasily for several minutes.

His concern eased at the end of that time. There was no pleasure in the woman's expression now. She was at the controls, with full responsibility for their lives, and she took the charge deadly seriously. She was also, he saw, more than capable of managing the vehicle at this rate, at least as long as the light held. He would have to take over again once Diamond set. They would have to travel without beams, and he did not believe her skill was the equal of that challenge. In the meantime, he had plenty to keep him occupied.

Once his meal was finished, the Ranger exchanged his ripped clothing for the spares they had brought in case of such need and removed three black disks from his pack. Each was six inches in diameter and two deep and consisted of two parts, a base and a grooved cover that fitted over it and could be moved into various settings in relation to it. These absorbed his complete attention for some time, and it was nearly dusk when he finally straightened in his seat and set them carefully beside him neatly stacked one atop the other. Then he prayed.

* * * *

When Diamond's light was nearly completely gone, Murchu gently touched the woman's arm so as not to startle her out of her concentration. "I'll take over from here. The next stop will be the spaceport."

"Good enough. I was growing a little tired."

"No wonder. You did a fine job of flying, Doctor."

She smiled but said nothing more until she had set the vehicle down and returned to the passenger seat. Her fingers brushed the topmost disk.

"What are these things?"

"Incendiaries."

"What!"

He laughed at her expression. "Stand easy, Doctor. They're harmless until activated. Even a laser beam through the three of them couldn't set them off as they now are."

"That is reassuring to hear," she said curtly, but she inched a bit away from the weapons all the same. "How do you use them?"

"Slip them into or onto cargo or in some likely dark corner of a building or starship, set the timer, and run on all burners."

She was quiet a moment. "Taigue?"

He knew that tone. Something was troubling the archopologist. "Aye?"

"What if we are wrong and those fighters are carrying some other cargo?"

"In that event, the Stellar Patrol will be guilty of incinerating two innocent vessels and their crews."

Banna stiffened, then she saw his grin and knew he had baited her properly. "You son! Someone should kick you from here back to Terra and out again."

He laughed. "Did you imagine I wouldn't look before scattering my playthings around?"

"Sometimes Navy personnel have to do appalling things—" she began apologetically.

His mood sobered. Twice in his career, he had been forced to make such a decision, to act on his own judgment alone in a situation where guiltless people would have died had he misread the few clues he had. On both occasions, he had been correct, praise the Spirit ruling Space, but never did he want to be put in the position of making such a choice again. With all his soul, he dreaded the thought of such weight coming down on him a third time.

"I'll do what I must, Banna. I've had to do that before, but rest assured I'll make every possible effort first to confirm I have the right targets before moving against anyone."

* * * *

The rest of their race was a waking nightmare for Banna Lis. Taigue allowed no lights whatsoever, and it seemed impossible to her that they could travel even a few feet, much less the whole course, without slamming into some obstruction or other in the black of Ruby's night. He was not happy himself. She could see enough of him to be aware of the tension gripping his face and body, and from the way he kept wiping his hands against his trousers, she knew they were sweating.

Whatever about his concern, the Ranger neither slowed down nor raised the flier until well after midnight. Then, almost without warning, he stopped and settled to the ground amid a cluster of boulders, none of them higher than the vehicle and few even that tall.

"This place won't screen us in the daylight, but we won't be needing protection then, whatever way the fight goes."

"It is still a long way to the port."

"Better than a mile, and with precious little cover along the way," he agreed, "but poor as it is, I couldn't recall anywhere better farther in. Besides, our opponents might hear us if we come closer in the flier."

Her eyes were on him. They were huge and scared for all her courage. "You do have a plan of action?" Whatever her fear, her voice was steady.

"In general. I have seen the place. That much is to our advantage. What I decide to do will depend on the stage they've reached in the loading, but I at least know where the fighters and the warehouses are and what the country around looks like." He stared into the darkness for a moment. "That's assuming we have anything left to do at all."

"We did not see or hear any starships lifting, and we were watching for that," the woman reminded him firmly. "Move out, Captain. Sitting here will only weaken our nerve."

"Whatever you say, Doctor."

She made herself smile and shake her head. "I wonder if Commandos feel like this before one of their missions?"

"Very probably. They do if they have a neutron of sense."

* * * *

A good part of Taigue's fear was centered around the approach itself. It was justified, though more because of its physical difficulty than the peril they faced for most of the way.

Ruby's nights were fiercely dark. That benefited clandestine work, but it also slowed their movements. Between the poor visibility and the scarcity of cover which forced them to crawl for long stretches, they were open prey to the subzero temperature and to their own taut nerves. Anything strange on a planet as dead as Ruby of Diamond had to be alien. They were not likely to be seen, but a significant noise could readily betray them. Sound carried far, and even though they were downwind of the port, any clatter they generated would probably reach the installation.

The Auroran bit her lip as she just braked a slide that would have sent her sprawling. Fortune was with them in that the ground was chiefly either solid lava or gravel so tightly fixed in its place that no conceivable normal movement of theirs would dislodge it, and there was little loose stuff for a badly placed foot or hand to set rolling, chiefly material dropped by the recent storm.

That was more than enough to bring disaster. She could not move through the night like a living ghost the way Taigue did. All too often, she sent one or more pebbles skipping, and at each such mishap, her heart seemed to leap into her mouth as it resounded through the night, to her ears at least, like the thunder during one of Aurora's spectacular queen storms.

Murchu was aware of every accident as well, but though he jumped inwardly each time, he made no show of his nervousness. He was not as deeply alarmed for one thing. Dead, Ruby was, but her night was not utterly still. The sounds around them were slight, barely perceptible, but they were present. The wind had not yet settled, and a great deal of loose stuff was being blown about with very similar aural effect to that of a displaced small stone. As long as no major disaster struck, they should be all right.

Banna was not doing so badly. Conditions were against her with the moonless darkness and the cold which left hands and feet numb and unresponsive, but she moved lightly, with a natural, feral grace which saw her through many a bad moment. She also learned extraordinarily quickly.

He did wish heartily that he had not felt it necessary to bring her with him, but he did not see he had any real choice about it. This was not the country near the abandoned stockpile. The flier would be a painted target once Diamond rose. Whatever shadow of a hope she was to have if he fouled his own part, she had to be well away from it. Besides, he thought defensively, this was night, and the chance of casual observation was almost nonexistent. Banna Lis was no danger to him, not at this point, and as long as she was not, he would keep her with him. If nothing else, having her nearby as long as possible would leave him easier in his own mind. He would at least know what was happening to her.

They continued on slowly but steadily, traveling by compass until they at last spotted light glimmering on the horizon, only a sliver at first, but it soon brightened and expanded. It came from the spaceport rather from Ruby's sunstar.

Noise, alien noise, came with the illumination, shouts and curses, the crash and clatter of heavy material being maneuvered without the aid of major automatics, the whir of a flier—all the sounds particular to a small, unmechanized, primitive spaceport. In this place and time, knowing what they did, the effect was unspeakably sinister, as sinister as the operation in progress there indeed was, but the Ranger-Captain's spirit soared. They were in time. He still had an enemy and a cargo on-world which he could hope to fight.

Chapter Twenty-Two

It was not many minutes longer before the off-worlders lay on their stomachs at the rim of the paved saucer of the planeting field itself.

Taigue gave one look over his shoulder. The two big rocks beside them afforded poor defense and poorer concealment, but they did not have a great deal of choice. Even were there better sites around, he would not have squandered the time needed to seek one of them out. Those two starships would probably wait until dawn to lift, since they did not expect trouble and that would be the course legitimate vessels would take, but they should be ready to go in a couple of hours or maybe less by the look of them. Probably they had enough of their deadly cargo already aboard to lift now if the pirates felt themselves to be threatened at all.

The Ranger studied the needle-noses carefully. There were no big floodlights in this port, but the fighters' hull lights more than sufficiently illuminated the two vessels.

There was no activity around them at the moment. That was taking place in spurts, if he reasoned correctly. With no cargo-handling machinery available, the entire process had to be managed by the nine pirates themselves, four of whom would be in the warehouse where the contraband had been stored. They would heft the various containers into their flier, which then would deliver its load to another four hands waiting somewhat sheltered inside the hatch of one of the starships. Upon its arrival and unloading, these would cart the crates to their places in the hold. They would transfer to their sister fighter when the next lot reached them, putting it on the second ship. Most likely, they were all taking turns driving their vehicle.

Taigue battled down the fear roiling through him. It had been useful, forcing him as it had to make his approach with the proper degree of caution, but with the time for action on him, he could not afford to let it cripple him.

Nine raiders. He had often faced steeper odds than that, but he had always had some sort of backup, at least one competent comrade upon whom he could depend, and never before had so much been riding on the outcome.

As he had done when he had moved in on the abandoned stockpile, the man drove all that from his mind, his sense of responsibility and his awareness of how intensely he wanted to survive this. Extraneous thought or emotion had no place with battle upon him.

There would be no escaping combat. He would avoid clashing openly with the renegades as long as he could, but some fighting was inevitable, whatever his hopeful words to his companion. He would just have to pray—and make sure—it did not come so soon and hot that he would not be able to complete what he had come to do.

His hand closed quickly on Banna's in farewell. Then he darted out onto the pavement. Keeping low to lessen the chance of skylining himself against the glow of the fighters' lights, he raced across the open space separating him from the nearer of the starships.

He should be all right. The darkness outside the circle of light was almost total, and his clothing was dark. Even should any of the raiders happen to glance in his direction, they were working in the illuminated area and would not be able to see anything beyond the brilliance cast by their ships' lamps. It was only when he reached that point himself that his real peril would begin.

The Ranger slowed as he neared his target. He had meant the assurances he had given Banna Lis earlier. He could not simply attach an incendiary to one of those crates and slip back into the night without confirming they did in fact contain the stolen chemicals, but doing it would hold him under the hull lights for an uncomfortably long time.

Boldness was his best weapon here. He straightened and strode purposefully toward the small pile of cargo still waiting to be loaded. He took care to keep to whatever shadow there was and to stay out of line with the warehouse door and the fighter's hatch, but anyone glimpsing him would find nothing furtive in his movements and would, fortune willing, take him for one of their own number.

He was not long in gaining the evidence he required. The crates were already marked with labels declaring their origin on Gamma in lettering large enough for him to read even before he came close to them.

All that remained was to choose the most effective nest for his charge. The contents of the boxes were not listed on their sides, but the thieves had solved that difficulty for him. Since they might conceivably be disturbed during the loading process, however unlikely that might be, the raiders had opened each crate to make certain they would escape with the correct proportions of the chemicals to ensure some significant profit from their efforts. It was a simple matter for him to lift the loosened lids and peer inside.

The first contained laboratory equipment of various sorts. He left that and tried the next.

This time, he smiled. It held long, slender cylinders. Liquid compounds, all bearing identifying labels. Some of them, at least, would add to the power of his initial explosion.

Murchu had hooked the deadly disks to his belt when he and the woman had quit their flier. Now, he lifted the one he had allotted for this task from its place and activated it. He quickly slipped it into the pharmaceutical crate, well back where a casual examination such as he had just given would not reveal it, and sauntered away, apparently toward the warehouse.

Taigue drew a steadying breath when he reached the shadows once more and stood still for a few seconds until his eyes had readjusted to the night, then he turned and hurried toward the second fighter.

His job would be more difficult this time. There were no boxes conveniently stacked outside the vessel. If the pirates were working as he reasoned they would be, they were loading their flier with material for this ship even now. He would have to board her and find his way to her hold, that or set his charge somewhere else inside the fighter and hope it had the power to take her down without the aid of auxiliary combustibles.

He did not relish either course. Federation Commandos were closely trained in the ways of their enemies' vessels and knew the insides of an Arcturian battlecraft as intimately as they did their own—or even more intimately. Exploratory Force agents had not been similarly well educated. He knew how to meet the armaments and overcome a pirate fighter's defenses in battle, but he had never been inside one or studied the plans by which most of them were constructed. Those were not standard in any event. The members of a wolf pack came from many different sources.

He would not be working completely blind, of course. A veteran space hound like himself would not be far off in guessing the basic layout of such a vessel, but that might not be good enough. He could not afford many miscalculations, however minor, once he did board, and none at all should the crew happen to return while he was within.

Voices! Taigue raced up the boarding ramp and leaped through the hatch, clearing the open lock a bare instant before the four raiders who had been working inside the first starship emerged and hastened down her ramp to retrieve the remaining crates.

He cautiously moved farther into the ship, seeking the core ladder, the universal mode of access to the various levels within small and medium-sized vessels.

How much time did he have? The pirates' flier had been inside the warehouse before he had stepped out onto the planeting field. The crew members in there must have nearly finished loading it by now, and when it was full, they would be coming here. Once they began work on this fighter, he would be trapped, hidden perhaps if his luck held, but unable to do more, and all the while, the timer on his first charge would be inexorably sliding toward its detonation point. He would then be faced with the unenviable prospect of activating the shorter fuse on the incendiary meant for this craft and remaining aboard until it went off, or of waiting for it to explode if he had already done so.

The Ranger-Captain found the ladder, but instead of descending to the cargo holds, he started to climb, making for the bridge.

He had spent the better part of a lifetime, boy and man, using such ladders, and he scrambled up this one in a matter of minutes. He was scarcely aware of the effort at all save that he pushed himself for speed.

The bridge was in the usual location, in the vessel's nose, as he had assumed would be the case. Murchu looked around the crowded cabin for a moment with real regret. This was probably the most efficient setup he had ever seen for the command center of a small, fast fighting starship. The Stellar Patrol, if not the Navy itself, could profit well from a close study of it.

There was no chance of that. The little battlecraft was as much death's agent as if she carried the seeds of some ghastly plague. His face hardened. It was not a clean death she represented, either, but a cataclysm of poison which neither the Stellar Patrol nor any surplanetary police force could hope to deflect before countless thousands had perished and countless more lives had been destroyed.

There was no hesitation in him. He knew what he was going to do. Swiftly, almost lightly, he gently worked the panel covering the drive controls loose with the tools which were part of every spacer's gear. There were no alarms or safeguards to counter, and it was the work of seconds to remove it. He activated and carefully inserted his second incendiary disk, then replaced the panel.

After a quick check to be certain he had restored everything to seeming order, the man made for the ladder, descending two rungs at a time. His fear of discovery sharpened with each second, and fast as he moved, he took care to make no noise which might be heard on the outside or by anyone working below.

When he reached the hatch level, Taigue reined his drive to escape and crept forward, inch by slow inch, listening for any sound announcing the raiders' presence either within the ship or outside.

Nothing yet.

He came to the lock itself. The field beyond remained clear, but the crew loading the other fighter were still outside, cursing and grunting as they struggled with the crate carrying their starship's doom.

Their progress was slow, so slow they seemed hardly to move at all, and his nerves tightened until it took the full grip of his will to hold him in his hiding place. Here, there was still a chance. If he made his break prematurely, he was a dead man . . .

They had it inside. Still he waited. He counted thirty seconds after the last sound from within had faded to be certain no backward glance would betray him, but after that, he shot outside and tore down the ramp until he was close enough to the ground to leap down without risking injury. Speed was needed. There had been only a little cargo remaining to be stowed aboard the first ship, and the pirates would be coming out again at any moment. They would hurry to this vessel to await the flier's next trip. If they were still outside when the ships blew, they had a good chance of escaping what was to come. The Patrol would then be able to sweep them up at its leisure for trial and nearly inevitable execution.

Murchu landed fairly upon his feet, steadied himself, and dashed for the protection of the darkness.

He stopped again as soon as he gained it. Away from the light, he was nearly blind.

His vision took longer to adjust this time but he made himself hold still until he could see well once more. When he was sure his eyes were functioning properly, he ran for the rim of the field, not to the place where he had left Banna but to the point almost precisely opposite it.

Only when he gained the target his mind had set did he allow himself to breathe freely, to relax for a few brief seconds. All too soon, purpose returned to him. His work was not finished yet. An unknown part of the stolen shipment remained in the warehouse, and while it did, there was always the chance, however remote, that one of the starships would survive his attack in sufficiently sound condition to be repaired and be able to complete her mission. There was also the possibility that renegades sent by the masterminds would arrive to take the load off before Stellar Patrol reinforcements could reach Ruby. He had to try to counter that slim risk as well.

Taigue's gloved fingers searched the pavement beside him until they encountered, as he had anticipated finding, a sunken latch, the handle of a square door set flush with the surface. He tugged at it gingerly lest it squeak or slam back too suddenly, but the Settlement Board maintained the service portions of even its outermost port facilities carefully, and it swung up noiselessly, bringing the nozzle of a hose with it.

The line stored inside unrolled easily. This spaceport was designed to meet the needs of the vessels utilizing it. Most of those were small with few hands, and so the fueling hose was light in weight, readily manageable by a single person. Its location was dictated by tradition, a convention followed in the construction of all such ports, particularly those like Ruby's which had no permanent staff, so spacers unfamiliar with the facility would suffer little delay if they planeted in need of emergency help.

This would be the only hose for liquid fuel. Nearly all newer starships were designed to be powered by the more stable solid compounds or had converted to them, and there would be a couple or three bunkers holding the more advanced fuels to answer their wants, but it was precisely the liquid's volatile qualities which he required now. If he could put a thin coat of it on those fighters, no human power would save them when the flames from the incendiaries and exploding chemicals reached their hulls.

The nozzle turned easily. It took him a moment to find the proper angle, but once he had that, the glistening, colorless stream it spat forth bathed first one and then the second of his targets.

Murchu turned off the spray. The warehouse still remained, but the threat it represented was not so great that he was willing to incinerate five human beings to destroy it. Little though they might merit the consideration, the Ranger-Captain was determined to wait until they were outside before firing the place, although he knew he would be drawing greater danger on himself by doing so. He had accomplished enough of his purpose that he could afford to take the risk.

Taigue unhooked his remaining incendiary and set it beside him after first altering its timer. He had not needed it and had brought it only as a backup, but it might still prove useful. Better to have it ready if he should require it.

Another worry loomed large in his mind now that he had a few moments to dwell on it, and he sniffed his gloves and clothes for any scent of fuel. If there had been spillage, the first spark reaching him would turn him into a torch.

To his relief, he detected nothing, though he had not expected to find any traces of the hazardous substance. The hose was fitted with a safety nozzle to prevent just such a mishap, and the half gale which was blowing was more than strong enough to catch loose drops and droplets even as they formed and whirl them away from him.

He shivered. The wind was damn cold, however well it was serving him.

When would those bastards come out? It had to be any moment now . . .

He did not hear his incendiary blow, but suddenly the side of the first fighter ruptured in a rush of fire and noise, a chaos sustained by a seemingly continuous series of explosions. The cargo was detonating with unexpected ferocity as the flames penetrated the crates and cylinders in the fiercely burning hold.

The entire starship was ablaze, burning with terrible heat. Murchu stared at her, scarcely believing the relatively minute amount of fuel he had used could have carried the fire to every part of her so quickly or burn with such awesome power.

He braced himself. He had timed both charges to go off within moments of each other.

The second fighter went up. There was no perceptible interval this time between the initial internal blast and total involvement, and the fury consuming her dwarfed that rending her sister. Within three minutes, she had toppled and was literally crumbling in upon herself.

Instinctively, the man flattened. What force in all space had given such instantaneous power to his charge? By rights, it should have taken longer to accomplish its ends, longer than the destruction being wrought on the other vessel. It had been placed on the bridge, after all, not with the cargo as his first had been.

He frowned. The bridge. That might explain it. If the concussion had activated the weapons controls, the laser banks might have fired, or if the command to lift had somehow been transmitted to the drive engines, the ship's own fuel could have ignited.

It was the last, he decided. One or more exploding fuel coils would readily account for the violence he was witnessing.

Murchu tore his eyes away from the hypnotic splendor of the blazing starships. The flier was racing to aid the four shaken on-site renegades in manning the foam hoses which were part of every spaceport's equipment. He could not see clearly how many were in it but hoped it was all of the remaining five.

He could wait no longer. The Ranger-Captain rose to his knees and sent a strong spray of the deadly fuel toward the open door of the building.

It fell short. He quickly adjusted the nozzle, but before he could try a second time, a blaster bolt sizzling within inches of his head sent him sprawling to the ground.

Others followed fast upon it. The pirates had seen him. They knew their fight to save their ships was hopeless, and they turned all their frustration and fury to the task of taking down the one who had brought this disaster on them.

They would soon have their will. The flames from the burning fighters threw the whole planeting field into clear, ghastly relief, and he was as visible as if Diamond's light filled the sky. His foes could scarcely have desired a better or easier target.

Chapter Twenty-Three

Banna Lis watched the Ranger approach the first pirate fighter and move on to the other after his work among the crates was done. Her fingers tightened on the grip of her blaster as he hesitated at the hatch. His worries were so reasonable she could all but read them as they formed in his mind, but she knew as well as he that he had no time for indecision. Those space vermin would be reappearing at any moment to fetch the rest of their cargo.

They were coming! Her heart nearly stopped and her breath did stop, but she saw Murchu vanish inside the starship's lock just as the first of his enemies emerged.

The minutes which followed were the worst she had known since she had sat powerless and terrified beside her dying husband, waiting for the help she knew must come too late. There were so many things that could go wrong, so much that might happen. So great was her fear for her comrade that she was completely unaware of the deadening cold or of the wind driving it. She was unaware even of herself.

Taigue came out at last, moving with a caution she much appreciated. He was in too great danger as it was without playing a shooting star.

To her surprise, he did not return to her but went instead in nearly the opposite direction.

Anger rushed up in her. Murchu had accomplished what he had come to do. He could now at least share the rest of his peril with her. What was the point of sparing her that? How much real chance did he imagine she had if he were killed, leaving her alone on an unforgiving planet with nine enraged renegades snapping at her fins?

Her resentment died as soon as it was born. The fighters were not blown yet. Until they were, his mission was not complete.

Mission? So it was, a military mission in all but the technicality of the service whose uniform he wore. He had to conduct it as he saw fit.

It was not long before she realized what he was about. Banna stared, fascinated, while her companion sprayed the vessels. The simplicity of the move impressed her, but its stark thoroughness horrified her. How readily a tool designed to aid spacers could be made to bring destruction upon them instead by someone trained to violence . . .

The warehouse was a logical, a necessary mark as well, but Taigue did not turn his hose on it.

Creation's Lord, she thought, he would get himself killed if he put this off until later. He had to be well away from the planeting field before the explosions started, or he was certain to be seen.

Knives of fear stabbed through her. He would delay all the same. He was without choice. This target was not imperative in the sense the two starships were. That being the case, the Ranger-Captain could no more fire it with those people inside than he could ignore it entirely. Either course would be completely alien to everything she knew him to be.

First one and then the other ship exploded. The woman partly buried her face in her arm to shield her eyes from the worst of the glare, but she dared not shut out all sight of what was happening on the field. She was close enough to it that the pirates might possibly stumble on her hiding place, and she had to be on the alert to withdraw or defend herself as the situation warranted.

She could not turn her eyes away, not completely. The scene was dreadful, but it was compelling, commanding her attention whether she wanted to give it or not. She had to watch this fury through to its end.

Although she recognized and despised them for what they were, the pirates' loss aroused the Auroran's sympathy and more so the desperate determination of their fight to save their doomed starships. To a space hound, she knew, his vessel was everything, not merely transportation and a means of livelihood but almost a friend, a lover. Her destruction could be more painful than a comrade's death.

Her attention swept back to Murchu. He, too, had hit the ground, but he was moving once more, coming to his knees to wield the hose again now that his target was empty of life.

Lis bit her lip. Probably empty. She could not make an accurate count of their enemies. The activity around the ships was too frenetic. Someone might be lurking at the entranceway where he or she would have good cover and an excellent view of the planeting field.

Her tongue moistened dry lips as Taigue released a stream of fuel. It fell too short. He would have to try again.

Banna gasped and barely choked back a scream. The Ranger was under fire, heavy fire, from the raiders. He had flattened out but had no cover, and with this kind of pressure, he would be cut down in a matter of seconds.

One of the pirates jerked erect as Taigue shot him, flinging his blaster into the air as he fell onto his back. The woman sighted her own weapon. The curs were bunched, and she had no trouble finding targets.

She selected one and fired. He dropped. Another went down a moment later as her next bolt burned home.

The remaining renegades realized they were caught in a crossfire and scattered, keeping low as Murchu had done and diving for cover, but she picked off another as he ran, and Taigue's weapon claimed a second victim.

The firing ceased. Their surviving foes had found shelter and were waiting to get an estimate of what they were facing before exposing themselves again to the ruthlessly effective attackers.

* * * *

Murchu seized the opportunity the lull provided and grabbed the hose once more. There was no error in his aim this time. The stream went straight through the open door and carried well inside. A second spurt followed, streaking along the ground and driving his remaining incendiary before it. In the next instant, the building had transformed into an inferno.

A line of furious energy whipped toward him, and he went down, writhing in agony, as a blaster bolt seared across his right hip.

Taigue retained his grasp on his weapon. Somehow, he kept shock at bay so it did not paralyze his mind and reflexes, and even as he fell, he rolled over to face his attacker.

He spotted her crouched by the wheel of the flier. As he watched, she prepared to finish him.

He sent a short burst in her direction to throw off her aim, then immediately released another, better considered bolt. That one struck true. The pirate fell forward, her face contorting and freezing as pain and death hit her simultaneously.

The expectant quiet returned once more. The Ranger knew he had good reason to distrust it and half rolled, half crawled until he was out of the lighted area. Screened by Ruby's black night, he would be able to take stock of himself in relative safety—unless one of the other renegades had seen his escape and struck before his sight had readjusted.

When his eyes began to work again, he twisted his body to look at the burn he had suffered as best he could. It was too dark to examine the wound itself, but he could see the charred stripe the raider's bolt had torn in his jacket and trousers.

Taigue did not think he was hit badly. The injury seemed to be a glancing surface strike with no depth. At least, there appeared to be no function loss. He had been lucky, he thought wearily. It had been a near enough thing. A few more inches higher, a bit farther in, and he would have nothing much worth mentioning left of his innards.

Heavy or light, the damn thing hurt like all the Federation's hells, and he was glad of this chance to get his breath back and brace himself before he had to fight again.

Noise! It was no more than a shifted pebble, but the sound seemed loud as an alarm to his stretched nerves.

Murchu spun about but recognized as he did so the whispered password his companion and he had arranged and responded to it in an equally low voice.

Banna raised her hand slightly as soon as he acknowledged her and wriggled her way over to where he lay. "We're safe for the moment," she informed him. "I was watching. None of them came out here."

The Ranger-Captain's fingers closed warmly on her hand, but he restrained himself from folding her in his arms. They dared not relax so far, although he wanted nothing so much in that moment than to press her close to him.

The Auroran brushed his face with her free hand. The mask was stiff to touch. His sweat had soaked it and was already freezing.

She wished she could get a proper look at him. Taigue Murchu was not likely to volunteer information about how significant he believed his injury to be or how much pain he was actually feeling, not at this stage, since they had no choice but to go on with the battle. The remaining pirates could not be left on the loose.

"How bad?" she asked. She had a right to some estimate.

"Not very. Mostly a surface sear, I think." His eyes swept the seemingly deserted spaceport. "There are still three we didn't take out. Did you see where any of them went to ground?"

She shook her head. "No. I was concentrating on you, but I am sure none of them left the port area. I knew enough to keep an eye on the perimeter. –Where could they have gone, Taigue? The whole area is pure chaos."

"Any number of places. Maybe they're in the sound warehouse. Maybe they dove into separate bolt holes. There are spots in plenty that would serve to shield one person. We'll rout them out once the fires die down. The cold should be making them a bit careless by then, and it'll be getting light. That'll help a lot as long as we don't permit ourselves walk into an ambush."

"Can we wait it out in the flier?" she asked hopefully. "The cold will be eating at us as well, and I would like to take care of that burn."

He peered doubtfully into the dark. "It would be a long crawl. I don't know if I could manage it, Banna."

He shivered visibly, and fear rippled through the woman. Was it the mark of fever or just a natural response to the slap of the wind. Determination firmed in her. "Maybe we could walk most of the way if we crouched low? I would be able to help you over the worst spots."

"It wouldn't be easy—"

"You will be sick by morning if we do not get your wound covered and shoot some anesthetic into it. That would put us at a disadvantage to state it mildly."

Taigue smiled at her blatant prodding. He would have to watch himself in the future, he thought. Banna Lis was a hard one to refuse.

This time, he had no intention of doing so. The archopologist was correct about his wound, minor as he believed it to be, and neither of them could take this cold indefinitely. Besides, if they left the vehicle unattended too long and their surviving enemies somehow discovered it, they would be in stellar-class trouble.

"You've convinced me, Doctor. Give me a hand up, and we'll see if this leg will take weight."

Murchu winced with the effort and stumbled when he did gain his feet, but the Auroran was strong in keeping with her height and gave him good support until he steadied.

After a couple of minutes of testing himself, he nodded. "No problem. I've felt better, but I've carried out assignments when I've been in worse shape than this."

"You would carry out an assignment if you were dead," she told him tartly.

The woman's eyes widened. "Taigue, up there! The Spirit of Space help us, look!"

Chapter Twenty-Four

The Ranger's head snapped in the direction to which she pointed.

He whitened beneath his mask. Two figures were standing on the roof of the blazing warehouse, one of them supporting the other.

The scene around them was something out of a nightmare or a madman's vision. The materials comprising the shell of the building were flameproof—they had to be to withstand the effects of potential planeting accidents—but the violent explosions rending the interior had holed the walls and roof in several places, and the skylight providing both light and emergency access to the place had been blown out. Flame was venting high and fierce through every opening like geysers from a savage hell. There was little safety anywhere on that roof, and soon there would be less or none whatsoever. It could not be all that much longer now before the whole or most of the expanse collapsed into the inferno beneath.

"What in the name of space could have moved them to go back in there?" the woman asked in stark horror.

"Who knows? Panic maybe, or they might have thought they'd have time to get something out to help finish us. Maybe they were in there all the time." Murchu studied the grim scene. "We'll have to airlift them off," he said decisively. "Can you find your way back to the flier by yourself?"

"Yes." There had been far too great a possibility she would have to retreat swiftly and alone for her to neglect to mark the course well in her mind.

"Fetch it, then."

"What about you?"

He studied the trapped couple. They had only a little time left. "I'm going to try to set up an alternate escape route across to the other roof in case you aren't able to return quickly enough."

"Taigue—"

"Go on. I have to do this."

* * * *

Banna Lis had scarcely left him when the concussion of a massive explosion drove him to the ground. A wave of heat and open flame shot out over him. It was far above, but his heart leaped violently, and he instinctively buried his face in his arms.

When Murchu looked up again, nearly the whole of the warehouse seemed to be cloaked in heavy fire. A great part of the left wall had been blown away, and he believed most of the roof, all its center, had fallen. The roar of the flames as they responded to the sudden surge of fresh oxygen was so monstrous, so utterly overpowering, he heard nothing of the great mass' fall.

At first glance, he thought the pirates were gone, but then he saw them, huddled at the very edge of the roof, trying to keep as far as their precarious perch would permit from the great tongues lashing the heavens so horribly near.

The Ranger's gray eyes were cold and hard as titanone. Banna would not be back in time now. Something had to be done for those people at once. Even if the place where they were standing did not collapse under them, either the ever-expanding flames would get to them or the heat itself would sear the life out of them. The temperature up there would soon match that of a starship's drive tubes if it did not already at the conflagration's heart.

He started running toward the sound warehouse, cursing the pain the effort wrung from his hip but grimly refusing to reduce his pace. He would have to ignore more than this if he was to bring the pair down.

Taigue took quick stock of himself and on the whole was satisfied. Major gymnastics would not be possible, but that would have been true in any event since at least one of the pirates appeared to be fairly seriously injured. He should be able for what he had in mind.

He froze that thought. There could be no questioning his capability. He would have to be able for it.

Murchu drew his weapon as he neared the door of the unaffected warehouse in case he should have to blast his way in but lowered it when he found the entrance unlocked. He did not reholster it.

Taigue hurried inside, sliding the door closed behind him to stop sparks or flame from gaining access to this building as well.

He moved cautiously once within, although the need for speed was like a whip driving him. One of the raiders was still missing. He was probably dead, a cinder, a crumbling lump of carbon in the inferno which might soon claim his two remaining comrades, but until that could be confirmed, he might be anywhere. He could be crouched in these shadows filling the empty warehouse, poised to strike . . .

The Ranger-Captain quelled that fear. He had to take the chance and act, or two individuals he might have saved would meet a dire death.

A long ladder hung from the building's skylight giving access to it. Returning his blaster to its place, he went to it and tested it for steadiness and weight, then nodded in satisfaction. It should serve. As in most such facilities, it was movable to permit its use for other purposes. It was also relatively light in weight, but whether light enough to be maneuvered as he must do, that was another question. Its length alone would be a problem, one magnified by the fact that he must handle it by himself.

He had no choice but to make the attempt. Murchu steadied the ladder against its supports and began to ascend.

It did not take him long to reach the top even with the pain the movement cost him. The catch holding the skylight closed was stiff, but after a couple of minutes, he freed it. That done, the whole lid swung up, allowing easy passage for his body.

The next stage proved as difficult as he had anticipated it would be. He had to haul the long ladder up and draw it out onto the roof through the narrow opening. It would have been no simple matter even with help, and if fortune should turn on him and he dropped it back into the warehouse, his hope of effecting the rescue was gone.

Taigue's concern with that possibility proved well nigh a premonition. He raised the ladder some five feet without mishap, but then he twisted too sharply in his struggle to continue lifting it and to keep it angled correctly at the same time. The sudden surge of pain ripping through his hip equaled that of the initial blaster strike, and he stumbled under the shock of it. His hands released their hold as they instinctively shot out to break his fall.

The ladder slithered back over hard-won feet. Murchu leaped for it, almost throwing himself down the skylight as he saw the topmost rung drop beneath its rim.

His right hand closed over it, stopping its fall with a shoulder-jarring wrench. He fought it back into place with the one hand until he could grasp it with the second as well. After that, he was able to secure it with relative ease.

The man rested for a few seconds, waiting for his body to stop shaking. The spasms were more the result of relief than of strained muscles, but even so, it was some time before he could gain sufficient control over himself to be able to continue his task.

Murchu was more careful of his movements when he set to work again. There were no more accidents, and although the struggle only grew the more difficult as it progressed, in the end, he had the ladder lying beside him on the roof.

Was he in time?

Aye, the pair were still there. They were very close to the edge now and were obviously contemplating jumping. The probable death they would meet on the pavement below was preferable to the one closing inexorably in behind them.

He shouted a warning to remain where they were and when he had their attention told them to move as near as they could to the corner, the point where the blazing building most closely approached its uninvolved comrade. Fortunately, they were on this side already, perhaps intentionally. They may have had some vague hope of leaping across the space between the two structures, but that would not have been possible even had both of them been sound.

He was near enough to recognize the Emirite woman Cass now. The man, whom she appeared to be more than half carrying, he had not seen before.

To her credit, Cass did not abandon her comrade, although the fire was pressing them hard. He was kin of hers, perhaps, or her husband. She had certainly shown no soft feeling for the Albionan Taigue had killed on their first meeting.

The Ranger felt unaccountably disgusted with himself. There would have been no point to that. The man had been dead, and a show of weakness or sensitivity to the fact would not have helped either him or the remainder of her party, nor would it have enhanced her standing among them.

He shuddered when he got a full look at the injured pirate. Anyone burned that badly should be dead. He probably was as good as dead, but the poor devil was somehow still conscious and still fighting to avert the remainder of his fate. Space scum these raiders might be, but no one dealing with or against them could term them plasmaspines.

Courage or no, would he be able to make the crossing? His whole left side was charred, blackened almost beyond anything recognizably human. The clothes were gone, and Murchu could see carbonized flesh curling, flaking away from seared bone. Both the arm and the leg, what remained of them, were useless or nearly useless.

The Ranger-Captain hoisted the ladder up and shoved it toward the imperiled couple. Miraculously, its end fell at their feet on the first attempt, and the woman drew it farther in to better secure it.

"Send him over first," he shouted when she straightened again. He did not relish the idea of having the relatively sound raider behind him on the roof while he tried to help her probably dying companion. She might well decide to sacrifice him to take out the man who was still her foe despite his present role. She would not be so inclined to make any such move against him—and chance throwing down her only avenue of escape—while the fire was still licking at her heels.

Cass nodded. This was precisely the way she would have handled the rescue, and she wasted no time protesting.

"Lie on your right side," Murchu directed the man. "If you can crawl at all, it'll help, but I'm coming over for you. Just try to hang on until I reach you. —Cass, help him. It'll be safer if you wait until we're completely across, but if you're too hard pressed, come on easily."

The Emirite signaled her agreement and maneuvered her companion into position.

Taigue groaned to see how narrow the ladder appeared beneath the injured raider. He would have to be a large man, he thought grimly.

That just about trebled their danger. They had no margin whatsoever for mishap or error.

The pirate struggled to move as instructed, but his ruined body could not respond. He advanced no more than a few inches before coming to a stop. He lay sprawled where he was, using what little strength he had to hold onto his narrow support, while death waited, poised to strike, behind and below.

Murchu started to creep toward him. His stomach lurched in pure terror as the ladder wobbled beneath him, but he kept his eyes open and compelled himself to continue moving forward.

Every inch gained required a battle against himself. Intellectually as well as instinctively, he disliked this slender, vibrating road, and something very basic inside him rose up violently against going any closer to the conflagration he himself had begun. His injury was acting as a brake on him, too. The hip was not functioning well, and he feared too much greater stress would cause it to give out or lock, that or jolt him into overbalancing himself. It was more than painful enough to do that if he made too sudden a movement.

The Patrol agent quelled that line of thought. It was no help and could cause him to freeze altogether if he dwelled on it too closely. He was also deeply shamed he had been considering his mere discomfort in the face of the other man's awesome suffering.

He reached the pirate at last and caught hold of his sound wrist. Cautiously, infinitely slowly, he began to draw him back along the ladder to the safety of the untouched roof. His mouth was dry with fear, and his heart slammed against his ribs with every lurch of their support. If his charge fell now, he was almost certain to go down with him.

He trembled in his heart to think of what this crawl could be costing the other and hoped he was feeling relatively little of it. There should be few nerves left alive to transmit pain in flesh so charred.

Murchu closed his mind to fear and sympathy alike and focused on the seemingly eternal task before him. So great was his concentration on what he was doing that he started almost disastrously when his boots struck a hard surface under the rungs instead of the familiar emptiness. He steadied himself, compelled himself to continue moving at the same careful, smooth pace until he was secure once more on the blessedly firm roof from which he had started out.

He did not pause even then but continued to draw the now barely conscious man along until he, too, rested on the hard, broad surface.

That done, he motioned to Cass to begin. She obeyed even as he did, with scarcely a moment, or so it seemed, to spare. A wall of flame was advancing on her, so closely the heat of it must have been singing her flesh, yet she had held to her place. The woman must have titanone for a spine, he thought numbly. He could not imagine himself holding out so long had their positions been reversed.

The nearness of the fire forced him to turn his attention back to the first raider. This warehouse was safe enough in itself, but they still were not, not this close to the blazing building. He dragged the man farther back so one of those gigantic tongues would not reach him should any of them chance to sweep out in this direction.

When he again looked back at Cass, he saw she had made good progress, but she was definitely having trouble. The Ranger-Captain realized both her hands and her knees were burned and perhaps a good part of her legs. He would have to help her, or she might go down.

Before he started for the ladder, he removed the male pirate's blaster and cast it over when he reached the edge of the roof. He wanted no chance of treachery while he was helplessly suspended above that drop, small likelihood as there was of it in this case.

Taigue mounted the makeshift bridge a second time. At least, his passage across it was less nerve-wracking. He was not a heavy man himself. Cass was lighter still and was in greater control of her movements than her comrade had been, so the ladder trembled less violently beneath them. Both also possessed a spacer's natural balance and long practice maneuvering in narrow spaces, and both of them were accustomed to the threat of imminent death. Even in these dire circumstances, neither was likely to give way to panic.

The pirate made no mistake. She advanced carefully, keeping her movements smooth and even despite the agony of her burns, which showed themselves to be more extensive upon nearer observation than he had first imagined.

The Ranger caught her wrist. Raw hatred blazed in her eyes, but she accepted the aid and support he offered. She knew she was unlikely to complete this crawl without his aid for all the strength of her will. The human body could be forced only so far, and she was close to the limit of her endurance. Murchu, for his part, felt no anger, although he read what was in her easily enough. If ever a man had earned Cass' hatred, he had after his work this night. He would sooner face it and what might spring from it than try to outguess an unnatural lack, or seeming lack, of response against him.

Slowly, they worked their way back to their refuge, where they would wait, out of reach of the fire itself but near enough to benefit from its heat, until Banna arrived with the flier to take them down. He did not want to chance replacing the skylight ladder and descending by that means. He and probably Cass would be able to make it all right, but he would not consider lowering the other pirate save in the case of extreme emergency.

At last, he once again felt the welcome resistance of a solid surface beneath his boots. Seconds later, he had gained his feet, and minutes later, he was steadying the Emirite woman, that and deftly slipping the blaster from her holster before she could move to stop him or draw it herself.

As he turned to dispose of it, a bolt crackled behind him, only inches from his head.

Murchu spun around, dropping to the roof and pulling his prisoner down with him. He cast himself over her as a shield even as he brought the blaster he had taken from her to bear.

A flier was tearing out of the night, firing as it came, but he realized even as he saw it that he was not its target. The needle-thin bolt struck the long knife in the hand of the male raider.

The injured man sat where he had raised himself, looking stupidly at his empty fingers. He made no effort to screen or defend himself. Taigue's blaster covered him, but the precaution was now unnecessary. What little fight had remained in him was gone.

That was not true of his comrade. Murchu felt her muscles begin to tense, and the fingers of his left hand closed roughly on her arm. He hauled her to her feet even as he sprang up himself, unbalancing the strike she had been about to make.

"Don't try anything more, either of you," he warned. "The next bolt goes home. It'd be pointless anyway. You're both badly injured, and there's no place for you to run."

Cass nodded, as much acknowledging defeat to herself as to him. For now, at least, she was beaten. "Why?" she asked dully, looking from the blazing warehouse to the ladder. "Why that?"

Taigue Murchu shrugged. "I'm Stellar Patrol. You people gave me no other choice."

Chapter Twenty-Five

The Ranger-Captain returned to Banna's flier. Now that the Regulars had arrived, it was the only place he could expect to find any peace around the spaceport, and he figured the archopologist would be there before him.

She did not disappoint him. Lis raised her hand in greeting when she spotted him and gave him a sympathetic smile as she opened the door to admit him. "Sit for a while and warm up."

"I'm not too badly off," he told her as he slid inside. "I just left the flagship."

He opened his jacket as the heat started to work on him. "That feels good all the same. I don't think I'd ever get used to Ruby's climate."

His eyes fell. Even last night, with all its terror and activity, he had not been able to forget the cold for more than a few minutes at a stretch except for the time when he had been on the roof in close proximity to the fire.

Banna held her hands before the heater. "That makes us a pair. Praise the Great Creator for Federation technology. Without it, I should find my job here very unpleasant indeed."

She studied Taigue critically. He was nearly as white as she was. Her eyes went to the bloodstains marking the tear in his jacket. They were large and dark although completely dry now. "How is the hip?"

"Sound out. My associates arrived with renewers." He smiled faintly. "The physician treating me wasn't overly pleased with the amount of stress I'd put on it, but there wasn't a whole lot I could do about that after the fact." His eyes closed for a moment. "Space, but I'm tired!"

"Little wonder after the night you had," she said sympathetically. "What about the other two?"

"They're well enough, better than could be expected. The man might live to stand trial if we can get him to a hospital with proper regrowth equipment rapidly enough. At least, he's not in pain. The renewer has already taken care of Cass." The missing raider was dead, blown to atoms in the warehouse when the crate he had been trying to open exploded.

"It does not matter much, does it, apart from easing their suffering?" she said stiffly. "They will both be executed."

"Within the next couple of months."

"So soon?" the Auroran asked in surprise.

"One of the places they hit on Gamma was a Navy facility. It's a military tribunal they'll be facing, not a civilian court. Not that the eventual outcome wouldn't be the same. They'll receive a just hearing, but there's no doubt of their guilt, and with the Arcturian Empire to quell, no one will have any patience with patent delaying tactics and even less with attempted circumvention on the part of their lawyers."

"Is there sufficient evidence to convict them with both the warehouse and the fighters gone? Our belief is not enough."

"Hardly, but don't forget their flier. That escaped basically intact, and it was fully loaded. As for the rest, you're underestimating Federation science. Our people can piece together a great deal from those wrecks. Besides, we've already begun to run a check on the pair. Rest assured, they're wanted in more than one place throughout the ultrasystem, either by the Patrol or by surplanetary authorities. There will be meat in plenty for multiple convictions in the unlikely event we fail to secure this one."

There was no triumph in his tone, Taigue Murchu took no delight in giving death, and any slow or consciously delayed means of causing it was repugnant to him. Had those two faced a less cruel end last night, he would have been strongly tempted to let them meet it instead of holding them over for this.

He sighed. He would not have yielded to it. The code by which he lived demanded that he try to take them living unless they were directly threatening him or someone else. Banna's seemingly implied rebuke was justified. He had delivered two people to certain death and had gone to a considerable amount of trouble to do it, yet to have left anyone, even vermin like these, to the flames . . .

Murchu covered his face with his hands. "Damn it to all the Federation's hells, what else could I have done? I'm a Patrol agent, not some sort of—"

Strong fingers closed on his arm. "Taigue, I am not challenging you."

His hands dropped to rest limply on his knees. "Sorry." His voice thickened. "I didn't enjoy turning them over, especially not the woman. She has backbone, whatever else she is. In point of fact, they both do."

"I know," Banna responded quietly. Her expression gentled. "You are spent, my friend. Knock out for a while. There is no emergency now. If your comrades have more questions, they can either ask me or jolly well wait a few hours."

"I could use about a week of sleep," he agreed. "I feel like I could drop off as I sit here with no effort at all."

Taigue took hold of himself. The Auroran might not be laboring under the aftereffects of an abused wound, but she was probably contending with worse. She had never drawn her weapon in anger before he had invaded her life, yet she had killed and killed more than once last night in his defense. He remembered the first time he had been forced to slay and cringed to think what she must be feeling now, with the crisis which had driven them both ended and all too much time for thought and memory. Her apparent serenity was part of her race, schooled into her from birth as the way to conduct herself while battling inner turmoil, but he knew she had assumed her air of cheerfulness chiefly for his sake. That did nothing to lighten his own already all-too-keen sense of guilt. He had not even thanked her yet . . .

His fingers brushed her cheek. She was pale beyond even her wont and still, but he did not think of a frozen sculpture now as he had that first night he had seen her. This woman was warmth, not ice.

"I owe you, Banna," he told her softly, "and I appreciate what giving me my life has cost you. Is costing you."

The archopologist smiled. "Someone has to take care of you," she replied, making herself speak lightly. "You Stellar Patrol agents do not seem to be able to look after yourselves very well when you are engrossed in some assignment."

He could not respond to her effort, although he recognized it for what it was. "It was my business to look after you."

"Your business was to do precisely what you did," Banna Lis told him firmly. She changed the subject abruptly. "Did you learn who is behind the robbery?"

"From the raiders? Not a hope of it. Even if they do know who ultimately hired them, which they well might not, space pirates wouldn't reveal that, not if you carved them into atoms. None of them would ever net a charter if those few unfortunate enough to be caught alive don't keep their mouths shut." He shrugged. "Why should they tell us anything? Talking won't save them, and silence is the only means they have of exacting any vengeance against us."

The woman's lips tightened. Failure was a bitter taste in her mouth. "Then it was all more or less for nothing. As long as we do not know who they are, they can always strike again."

"Not so readily. We destroyed or recovered all the contraband, and they're not going to find another haul like it free for the taking. Gamma and worlds like her won't be so careless again. On the offensive side, we do have one clue now."

"What clue?" the archopologist demanded eagerly.

"Pirate wolf packs are among the most diverse units in the ultrasystem. Even the bulk of Navy commands cannot match them for variety of composition. No race has a particular penchant for evil, and pirate craft are small. It's not common to find two hands from the same planet in any average-sized raider company unless they're blood kin."

"So?"

"Nearly every member of those crews was an Emirite. That's far too many for coincidence. It's not much to go on, maybe, but it does give us a start."

"Emir," she mused. "She has a reputation for being an unpleasant planet, I believe. To my knowledge, Aurora has little contact with her citizens."

"Be glad of it. No one enjoys a visit from one of their freighters," he informed her. "The crews are generally a rough lot, and they're far too ready to go to work with their whips."

"Will you be continuing on the assignment?" she asked after a moment.

"No. It's an intelligence job now, maybe even Navy Intelligence. Rank and file Patrol agents won't be involved, much less Exploratory Force people. We're not geared for work like that."

"You will have to testify, though?"

"Of course, most likely by deposition. I'm also facing a distressingly thorough debriefing." He looked at her somberly. "You'll be wanted on Deneva, too, to provide your deposition and for some detailed questioning. What will that mean to your own work?"

"A delay, but nothing more. I won't lose either time or funds. A citizen is not penalized by any Auroran institution for performing his or her duty."

"You've talked to the Settlement Board people, too? Feeding their animal cost you a good share of your supplies. That chap can eat."

"They are making arrangements right now to repay me. They are even making good for the fuel we burned, although, strictly speaking, our tearing around the planet on a military-class mission does not fall into their area of responsibility."

"I suppose they figure they owe you for helping save a few planets from a trashing."

"Maybe." Her eyes brightened. "They have already fetched in the cams. A team of their chaps arrived this morning with your Patrol friends." She shuddered. "The poor beasts! I am so glad they were nowhere near that battle."

"They're all right?"

"Sound out. The Board veterinarian reports you did a fine job on the bull's hoof, by the way, and thanks you."

"I'm pleased to learn the brute didn't attack me with cause." Taigue smiled as he said that. Banna's sympathy definitely was strongly oriented to the nonhuman denizens of the universe.

The light left him as the realization of everything he had brought upon this basically gentle woman returned to him with renewed force. She had killed for him, and she had watched him burn and kill. His heart twisted inside him, but he schooled himself to give no sign of his misery. He would not play on her pity on top of everything else.

How she must despise him, he thought with an inner groan. It was the strength of her character, her adherence to her word, to the avowal of love she had made before she had seen him at his grim work and had been forced to participate in it, which kept her sitting quietly beside him, as if nothing had changed between them.

He could not do that to her. The Spirit of Space knew, he loved her. He was sick with loss, but he had to release her. He must not bind Banna Lis to him, not now, when she could only shrink from him in her heart.

He steeled himself. There was no painless way of doing this and no point in delaying it. "Banna," he said quietly, "I know we've said things, let the emotion, the spirit of the moment, sweep us—"

The woman sighed heavily. "Well, you are right on schedule. I must give you that."

Taigue blinked, the rest of his intended speech scattering in his surprise. "Schedule?"

"With the self-sacrificial debris. Unless you have taken a second look at me and decided I do not provide a satisfactory alternative to your prototype ideal after all."

"No!" The Ranger tried to calm himself, to speak steadily and logically. "I'm trying to be reasonable. And . . . just. After all that's happened, I—"

"You figured I would be so shocked by what I have witnessed and experienced that my feelings for you might have altered?"

He nodded numbly. "Aye, something like that."

She looked down and was quiet for several seconds until his heart ached with the belief that she would confirm his fears. Strange, he thought miserably. For her sake, he was willing to release her, but he could not bear to hear her tell him his reasoning was sound.

The Auroran's head raised, and her eyes locked with his. "What happened last night revealed the extent of my feelings for you. I did not fight those pirates for the sake of unknown populations, Taigue Murchu. I fought them because they were attempting to kill my man. I would have gone after them with bare hands, nails, and teeth if I had lacked better weapons. –I know my mind, Taigue, and there is nothing in all the universe which will make me voluntarily separate from you."

Suddenly, her eyes fell, and she turned her face from him to stare blankly through the windshield. When she spoke again, her voice was so low as to be scarcely audible, and he did not know whether she was talking to him or to herself. "I loved Greg, Taigue. By all I revere, I did, but I never felt that way about him, that . . . protective—"

"Your profession was a peaceful one," he reminded her gently. "No one ever tried to burn either of you down, and you had no reason to fear anyone would ever want to do so. If you even thought about facing a pirate attack or other forms of violence, it was as an abstract possibility, just another of the many potential hazards to be considered by those voyaging and working on the rim. There was no sense of immediacy to spark a real reaction. Had you actually been threatened, you would have responded as you did last night. I know you well enough now to be sure of that, Banna."

"I wonder," the Auroran said, but she was grateful for his words and more grateful still because he had not tried to laugh off her suddenly born guilt or to make nothing of it by ignoring it. Her confusion and hurt and been very real.

Rather shyly, she extended her hand so his might cover it. There was a comfort and welcome in his touch that she craved in the wake of so much turmoil. "Thanks, Taigue. You are good for me."

The man bent and tenderly kissed her, not her lips but her brow. "I want only to shield you and be with you. If you had broken off—"

"You would have survived."

He smiled at her directness. "Survived? Aye, but now I know how bleak my loneliness was, and I would not have had the courage to try to seek out another to end it."

"No," she replied slowly. "I suppose you would not. I think we are both something of cowards in that respect. I shunned other involvements as well."

"Maybe our willingness to live in isolation is what's making this idea so acceptable to us."

The Ranger had spoken gravely, but his eyes were sparkling, looking more like sunlight shimmering on a windswept sea than ice or cold steel.

Banna responded in kind. "How do you figure that, Captain?"

'We won't have to surrender our solitary habits. Sure as space is black, I won't be around a whole lot."

"Good. Then you won't miss me so much."

Murchu laughed heartily. "I had forgotten that your profession is as bad as mine when it comes to accommodating a mate. –I shall miss being with you, though, and I fully intend to fulfill my responsibility as an agent of the Exploratory Force by checking on your progress regularly whenever you're in this Sector."

"Most of my work is here," she told him, "and I will hold you to that. I am always short of good hands, and you know I am not shy about putting an able man to work."

Banna saw the light go out of him, and her own mood sobered. "What is it, Taigue?"

"It won't do, Banna." He was hurting and this time made no effort to conceal his misery. "That might literally be the only time we'd get to spend with each other. Aurora's too far to reach on one of my furloughs, and both of us are too bound to our callings to pack it in. That wouldn't work, either, not for long."

The woman was so relieved she sagged against the seat back. "You are the worst worrier in the Federation, Ranger-Captain Murchu. I can base out of Deneva as readily—"

"If you think I'd allow you to do that, you're riding a comet's tail to the next galaxy. You have kin whom you love."

"Oh, do be quiet," she snapped irritably. "You do get furloughs even if they're too short for gadding about the inner systems, and I can pace my work pretty much as I choose. We will have time to share, and I will be able to go home to see my family and take care of any business that arises frequently enough. It is a move I was considering anyway. Archopology is a huge, complex field, and we all specialize. I concentrate on fairly newly discovered, virginal or nearly virginal digs, and most of those are located on or near the rim. It only makes sense that I should situate myself close to them, if only to save on travel time and expense. I have been lazy leaving the comforts of home and the convenience of being near the Institute and my publisher. Marrying you provides just the kick in the fins that I needed."

She smiled. "It gets lonely working by oneself for weeks at a time. I shall look forward to your visits." Mischief danced in the black eyes. "Even if they do not prove quite as exciting as this one."

He did not respond as she wanted but rather tensed as if in preparation for battle.

Banna looked around her in alarm but saw nothing out of the ordinary. She turned to him. "Taigue?"

The Ranger gripped himself. He drew a long breath. "Sorry," he muttered. "Someone just stepped on my grave."

"What?"

He was himself again and knew he must give her an explanation. "It's an expression of my subrace. A premonition. –I had the feeling as you spoke that trouble may follow us. It's enough a part of my life that the warning might be real." His face hardened. "I don't want to risk you again."

The archopologist shook her head. "You do tend to see her death in the birth of every star, do you not? —We Aurorans say everyone has reason to grumble at fortune now and then but it is rank foolishness to rail against challenges which have not yet been issued since they may, in fact, never come."

Murchu relaxed. He was embarrassed now by his show of nerves and gave her a sheepish grin. "You Aurorans sound like wise folks."

"Inner-system fops though we be?" she teased.

"Aye. There must be some sound raw material in you somewhere, I guess."

He leaned back and shut his eyes. It was good to sit here, quiet at last and with the woman he loved beside him, as he hoped to have her beside him for all that remained to them of life, aye, and beyond this life if the beliefs they both held proved sound. He willed the dark feeling of a few moments before to fade. It was a battle sense in him, an old comrade which had served him well in the past. He could not be such a fool as to discount it, but for now, he was content to let its warning ride.

Taigue's head turned slightly, and his eyes opened once more so he might see Banna. He felt strong again, able to manage both fear and that which sparked it. Peril and trouble might and probably did lie ahead. If so, they would have to meet them. He had done the same all his adult life. The only difference now was that he would be guarding, treasuring, a special individual and not merely laboring for the welfare of strangers and for an abstract ideal.

Banna's fingers twined with his. There was strength in them, as there was strength in the woman herself, and the courage rose in him at her touch, waxing high even as did his love for her. Whatever challenges fate chose to throw against them, those they would meet and overcome.

His head raised. He and Banna Lis could face anything as long as they stood together. They had proven that last night, and the Spirit ruling Space willing, they would continue proving it through all the time ahead of them.

About the Author

Pauline (P.M.) Griffin was born in 1947 on a quiet tree-lined street in Brooklyn, NY. The daughter of Irish immigrant parents, she arrived fully equipped with an Irish love of storytelling as well as a passion for accuracy and research.

Initially breaking onto the science fiction scene with her twelve-novel series "Star Commandos," she rounded out her career by publishing thirty science fiction and fantasy novels as well as twelve short stories and a host of nonfiction pieces, winning two Muse Medallion awards and Editors' Choice for Excellence awards.

Pauline always loved the natural world and the animals that filled it, and she infused all her stories with the same wonder. She lived quietly in Brooklyn with annual visits to her beloved Ireland to refresh her creative drive, but in many ways she also lived in realms beyond the stars and in magical kingdoms of mystery, fighting epic struggles and engaging with heroes and villains. She remained in Brooklyn with her cats and tropical fish until her death in 2020, but her literary legacy continues throughout the world.

Now Available!

KEVIN D. RANDLE'S
ALL-ACTION SPACE COMBAT SERIES
JEFFERSONS WAR

For more information
visit: www.SpeakingVolumes.us